I0551488

Praise for Holly Jacobs

Just One Thing

"Just One Thing is an emotionally compelling page-turner. I could not put it down."
—JoAnn Ross, *New York Times* bestselling author

"This poignant story about new discoveries, hope, and love is truly unforgettable."
—RT Book Reviews

Carry Her Heart

"An unforgettable story of unconditional love."
—Fresh Fiction

"Carry Her Heart is a beautiful story of love and friendship. And, Holly Jacobs' message of love is strong and touching."
—Lesa's Book Critiques

These Three Words

"A heart breaking love story with exceptional scenes... Highly recommended."
—Obsessed Book Reviews

"These Three Words by Holly Jacobs is about rediscovering love, even during the toughest times."
—Harlequin Junkie

Hold Her Heart

Hold Her Heart

Words of the Heart, Book 3

HOLLY JACOBS

Also by Holly Jacobs

Just One Thing
Christmas in Cupid Fall

Words of the Heart Series
Carry Her Heart
These Three Words

Dedication

To Kelsey! I promise; there's a happily ever after!

Sometimes home isn't just a place . . .

I am not your birth father, nor am I the father who raised you, but you are part of me. And when you find Pip, you'll find me.

You'll find us.

And when you do, there will be no shock of recognition; there will only be a welcome home.

For wherever we are, you have a home with us . . . you are part of both of us.

And we'll be waiting for you.

—From *Carry Her Heart* by Holly Jacobs

Prologue

Ned Chesterfield was done waiting.

He stood on the front porch of the unfamiliar house, in an unfamiliar town, feeling uncharacteristically uncertain as his hand froze mere inches from the door.

He knew that once he knocked, Pandora's box would open wide. There'd be no undoing it.

He also knew this was not what Pip wanted. More than that, she'd specifically told him not to come here. Ned also knew Pip could forgive him almost anything, although he wasn't sure she'd forgive him this.

But he'd decided that was okay.

If Pip never forgave him—if she carried a grudge for the rest of her life—he could live with that.

What he couldn't live with was a world without Pip in it.

He didn't hesitate any longer. His hand came down on the door. He prayed Pip would be mad at him for a very, very long time.

Part One: September

Chapter One

There was a scene in Tolkien's The Hobbit *where the dwarves all arrive unexpectedly at Bilbo's. It's chaos as he tries to play host to these unexpected guests. Felicity had always laughed as she read the scene—and she had read it many times.*

It wasn't until she opened her front door and found the entire team on her porch that she began to feel a certain sympathy for Bilbo. As she looked at the team's faces, she realized an unexpected truth: you can never tell what's waiting for you on the other side of the door.

—*Felicity's Folly*, by Pip

I heard someone knocking on the door. It was amazing that I managed to hear it because Carey was practically shouting.

"So what you're saying is it's over?" he asked loudly for the umpteenth time, giving his absurd blond ponytail a flip back over his shoulder.

I didn't bother to answer his question because I'd already answered it multiple times. Yes, that's what I was saying.

And I'd kept saying it.

Once I even said, "hell yes." Carey simply wasn't hearing me.

"Someone's at the door," I said instead of answering him yet again.

I was almost grateful that someone was interrupting this fight. I hoped it wasn't a neighbor here to complain about Carey's shouting. Mrs. Carmondy was very particular about noise levels. Once she scolded me because I had a group of mourning doves on my roof and they were causing a racket.

I'm pretty sure that a group of mourning doves is a bevy, but I'd have to look it up to be positive. I'm sure that a group of ravens is an unkindness. I'd always loved that term. *An unkindness of ravens.* It's not that I was a bird expert, but I found the group names fascinating, and thinking about them was easier than dealing with Carey.

"I'm getting the door," I announced and walked toward the front of the house.

"Leave it," he said. "Let's finish this. What you're saying is it's over?"

I turned back toward him. "Fine, Carey, let's finish this. I can finish it in four words, and I'll still have time to get the door. It. Is. Definitely. Over. *We* are most assuredly over. That's what I've been saying for days. Now I'm saying all that and also adding two more words, *get out.* Move out. Pack your stuff and leave."

"Where will I go?" This time it wasn't so much a shout as a whine.

How on earth had I ignored his propensity to whine for the last eight years? "You are a twenty-eight-year-old man. I'm sure you can figure something out. Maybe your girlfriend will let you move in with her?"

"I told you that she's not my girlfriend," he said. "It was just once. I told you that. You've been distant lately, and you've ignored my needs. Jocelyn was there for me. But it was only that once. I just made that one mistake."

"No, the mistake was mine. I'm rectifying it now. You need to pack up your stuff and get out by tonight. You don't have much, so it shouldn't take long."

I'd bought the house and most of the things in it. Carey had his video gaming system, his clothes, and not much else.

"I want . . . ," he started. That was Carey's favorite way to start a sentence. *I want. I need.*

Well, *I* didn't *want* to stay to hear the rest of it. I could hear another knock at the door, and I headed toward it.

I was so over Carey

I peeked out the window at the top of the door. I didn't recognize the man on the porch. I was thankful it wasn't a neighbor.

The stranger had a nice face. The kind of face that said you can trust me. His short hair was brown—very brown—with just the merest hint of gray at his temples.

I opened the door. I couldn't quite manage a smile, but I tried not to look annoyed. After all, the fact that I'd wasted the entirety of my adult life on Carey was on me, not on the stranger at my door. "Hi, can I help you?"

For a moment, he simply looked at me as if I were a long-lost friend. He whispered, "Siobhan."

I nodded. "Yes. Siobhan Ahearn. Can I help you?" I asked again.

"I hope so. You see—"

"Ban," Carey called. "If I leave I'm not coming back."

I turned back to Carey. "Good. That's what I've been trying to say. Go. Don't let the door hit you in the butt on the way out. Oh, and don't come back." I turned back to the stranger on my porch. "I am so sorry. You were saying?"

"Ban?" the stranger asked, homing in on my nickname and ignoring the fact that he'd been thrust in the middle of a fight.

I might not be able to answer any of my own questions about why I'd stayed with Carey so long, but this I could answer. People always found my nickname a bit disconcerting. "My name's

Siobhan. It's pronounced Shove-on, and if I lived in Ireland, I'd probably have a better chance of someone—anyone—knowing that. Every year on the first day of school, some teacher would stumble over it. I was in fifth grade when Mr. Lewis said, 'Ceo-ban.' The kids picked up on it and I was Ban from then on. It drove my mom nuts. She said Siobhan was a perfectly good name, and she hadn't imagined that anyone could find a nickname for it. She didn't count on my classmates. I was simply thankful I got Ban. Bryce Jazak didn't fare as well."

"Oh?" the man asked.

"Lice. He went through grade school as Lice." I'm not sure why I told him that, other than I was thankful to have a reason to be at the door.

I heard slamming coming from somewhere in the house and knew I was yammering at this stranger in order to avoid Carey. I just wanted him gone, not the gentleman on the porch but Carey. I wanted this drama to be over.

I was ready to move on to a new chapter in my life. Even though I didn't know what it would look like, I was sure it had to be better than this.

"Plus, I always told my mom that Ban is better than having people shorten my name to Shove," I added in a lame attempt at a joke. I could hardly manage a chuckle myself.

The man winced and I figured it was a really bad joke.

"Sorry. I'm sure you didn't come for a lecture on my name."

He offered me up a forced smile. "Hey, with a last name like Chesterfield . . ."

His name brought back sweet memories of days spent curled up on a blanket in the tall grass in my grandfather's field, reading. I loved the feeling of being hidden from the real world as I escaped into a good book. "You're named after a sofa?"

He nodded. "Ned. Ned Chesterfield."

"When I was a kid, one of my favorite books had a character named Coach Divan. It mentioned Chesterfield sofas in it. I had to look it up. They called him Coach Couch. Sometimes even Couch Couch." I was sure the book was still packed up in the attic.

Carey claimed my books collected dust and he was allergic. Well, I wasn't allergic to anything. As of tonight, after he moved out, I might not dust for a month just to prove a point.

A mental image of the Charlie Brown character wafting dust lightened my mood. Yes, I would *Pigpen* it for a few weeks at least.

I noticed that Ned Chesterfield wasn't smiling. He made a face I couldn't quite interpret, so I didn't even try. "How can I help you, Mr. Chesterfield?"

"Ned, please," he said, still wearing a bemused look.

"Ned," I echoed. We were still speaking through my screen door. I didn't have any more idea of what Ned wanted than when I'd first opened the door. I was pretty sure he wasn't planning on anything nefarious, so I stepped out onto the porch.

He was taller than I was but not uncomfortably so. I didn't need to crane my neck to look at him. And as I looked, I noticed his expression—he looked as if he were in pain.

"This is difficult," he said. "You see, I'm here about your mother."

I felt my heart constrict. If he knew my mom, maybe it wasn't my bad joke but my mention of her that made him wince.

I repeated, "My mother? I'm sorry to have to tell you that she passed away eight years ago."

And eight years later, saying those words still hurt.

I missed my mom. It was an ever-present hole in my life. I'd gotten used to it and even learned to live with it. At least most days. Some days—like today—I wanted her so badly I ached with it. I wanted her to wrap me in her arms and tell me everything would be okay.

I could almost hear her. She'd tell me that my time with Carey wasn't wasted. *Every experience has something worthwhile to teach you. Something you can carry with you into the next chapter of your life,* she'd say. I was certain about this because she'd said those words, or something close to them, so many times. Then she'd tell me again about how she'd wanted a baby so desperately and how much she'd suffered when the doctor had told her that she'd never conceive.

But Siobhan, it was such a blessing in retrospect because all along you were the daughter I was meant to have. Every piece of pain we suffer brings us a gift. You were my gift. The greatest gift I've ever received.

For the life of me, I couldn't figure out what life lesson Carey carried, other than I should avoid dating men like him in the future. And certainly he was a warning not to live with a guy like him again ever. Maybe I shouldn't live with anyone again. I sometimes feel I'm much better on my own than when surrounded by people.

As for gifts, I wasn't expecting to find one of those on my porch waiting for me. Instead, I'd found this stranger and had to deliver painful news.

"I'm so sorry," I said. That summed up my feelings about everything that was going on today.

"No, I'm sorry," he said. "I should have been more clear. I'm here about your biological mother. I met her on a front porch, too, you know," he added as if the memory were so strong that he didn't have a choice but to share it.

Another loud Carey-induced noise didn't faze me in the least now. At the mention of my biological mother I froze. "How? What?"

"Listen, she didn't send me. She doesn't know I'm here." Ned spoke quickly, as if afraid I'd turn around, go back into the house, and slam the door on him.

"She needs you. You're her last best chance." He stopped there, as if saying those five words caused him physical pain.

"I would never have bothered you if she had any options left," he continued. "And she will never forgive me for bothering you now. I've decided that I can live without her forgiveness, but I can't live without her."

His words sank in. *Last best chance. Can't live without her.*

"She's sick?" I asked.

He nodded. "I wanted to bring you the whole of your story, but it's not mine to tell. Hell, even this much isn't mine to tell. I know she'd say I was guilting you into helping her. I probably am. But I brought you this."

He thrust some papers at me. I glanced at them. They were obviously copies of some smaller handwritten pages. I took them more out of reflex than because I wanted them. I wasn't sure what to do with this man on my doorstep and some phantom biological mother who needed me. A birth mother who was sick.

I could see the anguish in Ned's face, and I knew that he loved her.

Truly loved her.

"Ban," Carey hollered.

I didn't respond. I looked at this man whose love was written on his face. There's no way to quantify or measure love, but if there were, Carey's love for me wouldn't have measured up to Ned's love for my biological mother.

"My wife spent years writing a journal to you," he said. "It's in your chest with all the other letters and gifts. I copied just these few pages. I wanted you to know at least this much. I came here not to force a meeting but to ask you to consider having the tests done."

"Tests done for what?" I finally asked.

I wondered if I should be crying. I hadn't cried about Carey, and here I was hearing about the woman I'd always wondered about, and I still felt nothing. It was as if all my emotions were balled so tight that none of them could get through. Not pain. Not fear. Not empathy. Not . . .

I had nothing inside me to give to this man who was pleading his case. So I stood, feeling shell-shocked, clutching papers I didn't think I wanted.

"Your biological mother, my wife, needs bone marrow. She's on the national donor registry, but so far there's no good match. She doesn't have siblings, and her parents aren't viable matches, which isn't surprising. But you could be. The doctors said that it would be a long shot. Kid to parent transplants aren't the norm, but a long shot is better than no shot."

The woman I'd always imagined wasn't someone who was sick. I'd imagined her with a large family. I'd wondered if she had ever thought of me . . . if she ever regretted giving me away.

I loved my parents and owed this woman I'd never met for that. By giving me away, she'd given me such a happy childhood. She'd given me to parents who treasured me and made sure I knew that I was loved every day.

"She isn't asking. She wouldn't ask. You need to understand that much. That's not who Pip is. She's someone who gives more than she'll ever take. But I *am* asking. I'm not nearly as generous as she is. Standing here right now, I realize just how selfish I am. And still I'm standing here. I'm not asking, I'm begging."

"Ban," Carey bellowed.

Ned reached into his pocket. "I know I've totally botched this, but here's my card. If you don't call, I won't bother you again. But Siobhan, you have to know, Pip never forgot you. You might not know her, but she built a life around you, and she's never stopped hoping that you'd find your way back to her."

With that, Ned Chesterfield turned and walked toward a car that was parked in front of my house.

"Ban," Carey said from behind me. "I don't want to do this."

I turned. "Tough. I'm going out for coffee. I'll be home in two hours, and I'd like you to be gone. If you've left anything, I'll send it to you later. Leave your key."

I grabbed my purse, stuffed the papers Ned had handed me into it, and walked down the block to the coffee shop. I thought about sitting inside, but I couldn't face running into someone I knew, so I ordered a coffee, took it down a few more blocks to the park, and found an empty bench.

I set the coffee down and pulled the papers out of my purse and realized that my hands were trembling. It was as if all the emotions I couldn't let myself feel had at last found an outlet. The paper actually rattled. I placed the sheets on my lap and took a deep breath.

I'd spent so much of my life imagining this woman, and here was something from her.

Ned had said that his wife had never forgotten me.

I hadn't asked if he was my father. I hadn't asked anything. But I was pretty sure from the way he spoke that he wasn't.

After a few minutes, I felt calm enough to look at the papers. They were a letter.

Dear Amanda,

Merry Christmas. It's evening now, and you were on my mind all day.

I bought you a car charm this year. I wonder if you're driving. If you are, be careful. I worry. I'm sure your mom and dad do, too.

I spent the day with my parents and a man I care about. At first I worried that I didn't feel the same passion for him that

11

I had felt for your father, but I've realized that I'm no longer a child and maybe a quiet caring is better.

You're sixteen now. I was sixteen when you were born.

My mother had written this when I was sixteen? Twelve years ago.

Some kids hated high school, but I'd loved it. Every moment of it. I'd had such a carefree childhood. But here was my biological mom telling me that she'd had a baby at sixteen.

I'd never blamed her for giving me up for adoption, but suddenly I realized that my biological mother had been just a kid when she had me. Would I have been equipped to make such a big decision? I didn't think so.

I tried to concentrate on the words as I read on.

My biological father had denied I was his. His name was Mick Grant—so Ned wasn't my biological father—and he played basketball. My biological mother had been a geek.

She'd gone to stay with an aunt in Ohio to have me.

She'd handpicked my parents and still had their letter . . .

I haven't read it in years, but they described themselves as normal and average. Your father was a professor and your mother was an elementary school teacher. They sounded like my parents, and I knew I couldn't give you a greater gift than parents who were as wonderful as mine.

I caught only a glimpse of them as they picked you up. They looked normal. Bland even.

Until the nurse handed you to your mom.

At that moment, they were transformed. Your mom was so beautiful. They were head over heels in love with you. And in that split second, I knew they were meant to be your parents.

And so I let you go.

But that briefest of glimpses has been something I've held on to all these years.

I hope they were—are—as marvelous as my parents are.

I started to cry. My parents had been marvelous. They'd loved me unconditionally and had supported me. Always.

After my mother died, my father limped along, half of a whole for a long time. Then he'd found Margo.

I know some people feel bitter toward stepparents, but Margo had never tried to take my mother's place with me or with Dad for that matter. She'd offered me friendship, and over the years I'd come to count on it.

My biological mother had gotten her wish; she'd given me a wonderful family. I thought about what my mother had said, how she'd suffered thinking she'd never have children. But when she'd adopted me, she'd known that she was always meant to be *my* mother.

My biological mother had now said the same thing.

I kept reading. As the copied letter ended, I was crying even harder.

It's midnight, Amanda. Another Christmas is over. I hope it was a wonderful one for you. I hope it was filled with love, laughter, and family.

Know you've been in my thoughts all day. You're in my thoughts every day.

Love,

Piper

I didn't have a tissue so I wiped at my face with the back of my hand. And suddenly what Ned had said really sank in. The woman who'd given birth to me and had written this letter so full of love—yes, that's exactly what stood out in her letter: love—this woman was sick. I was her last best hope, he'd said.

There was a scrawled note after the photocopied pages.

Siobhan,

Your mother wrote an entire journal to you over the course of years. She talked to you about so many things. I pulled this one section out of context. One reason is if you never come see us, you at least have your birth father's name. And though the journal excerpt doesn't make it clear, your mom is Piper George. She's Pip to her readers.

I'm sure you noticed how she addressed the note . . . Dear Amanda. *She didn't know your real name until I found you your senior year of high school. She held you for an hour after you were born and in her heart, you were always Amanda. She doesn't say it here, but she called that name as the nurse handed you to your parents. The fact your parents gave it to you as a middle name, well, it says something about them. I'm hoping their generous spirit is something they instilled in you. I hope you call me and try to help Pip. She'd be the first to say that you don't owe her anything. I'd say you owe her everything, even if you don't know it.*

If this is the only contact we ever have, know she's loved you and thought of you every day of your life. And know that you've always had a home with us, a family with us, even if you never knew it.

Love, Ned

I'm not sure how long I sat there after I finished Ned's letter. I know I never drank my coffee. My mind went in circles.

Piper George.

My biological mother was Piper George. She was the author, Pip.

I'd grown up reading her books. Now she was sick. She needed me.

Her husband loved her.

I reread the letters from Piper and Ned, and sometime after that, I walked home.

I don't remember walking home.

I did notice that Carey's car was gone, and when I opened the door, I saw his key on the foyer table. I waited to feel relief, or regret, but all I felt was anxious to find my books. I didn't check to see what Carey had taken with him. I simply went up to the attic and started tearing through boxes. I finally found them under a box of Christmas decorations.

Julie and Auggie.

Terry the Terrible.

Beautiful Belle.

The Hunt for Bigfoot and Other Wonders of the Eighth Grade.

B Is for Bully.

These books were old friends.

When I was younger, Pip had been my favorite author. She'd seemed to understand what school was like. I remembered reading *The Hunt for Bigfoot and Other Wonders of the Eighth Grade.* I'd been that girl. Tall. Gangly. And in a sea of developing friends I was as flat as a pancake.

I'd told my mom that I was pretty sure I had some horrible disease. I remember that she'd said *things happen in their own time,* and then she'd bought me Pip's book. As a teacher and an avid reader, she'd always felt that all the answers to all the world's questions could be answered in the pages of some book.

For a moment, I thought I'd start with that book, but then I spotted *Felicity's Folly.* I flipped to the front of the book and found the dedication.

"For Amanda."

15

Clutching the note and the book, I cried again for the mother I'd lost and the mother I'd inadvertently found. I cried for Ned, who wore his heart on his sleeve as he begged me to help Piper.

I didn't cry over losing Carey.

Chapter Two

"Every epic journey starts with just one step," Patty said.

"Then maybe it's a good thing I have such big feet," Eileen said.

"Why?"

"Because I'll get to where I'm going that much sooner."

—*The Hunt for Bigfoot and Other Wonders of the Eighth Grade*, by Pip

I stayed up all that night and reread every Pip books I owned. Each one was dedicated to Amanda.

I traced each letter of my middle name. I wondered about this woman who'd given birth to me and then had given me to my parents. She's obviously thought about me. According to Ned, she'd thought about me often.

When I woke up that afternoon, I called Ned.

Now, three days after breaking up with Carey and finding Ned on my front porch, I was in my car heading east on I-90, driving toward Erie, Pennsylvania. The autumn leaves made the drive picturesque, but it was the occasional view of Lake Erie that drew my attention.

Piper and Ned lived in Erie, on the shore of the same Great Lake as my Port Clinton, Ohio, home.

17

My parents had taken me to Erie one summer when I was a teen. We'd stayed at a cottage on the peninsula, and I'd spent a long weekend swimming in that lake and boating through its lagoons. And as I vacationed all those years ago, my birth mother had been in the same city, thinking about me.

When I was growing up, I'd noticed every redheaded woman and wondered if she was my biological mother.

She could have lived anywhere. Europe, the West Coast, Alaska. In reality, she'd lived a short drive from my home.

I'd visited her city as a child.

The day after Ned's visit, I'd gone and talked to my dad. He'd been just as supportive as I knew he'd be. "You have to get the test and see if a match, sweetheart. Even if it's a long shot, it's still a chance. Your mother would expect nothing less from you."

I knew that Mom would have been the first one to help me pack a suitcase. Mom was the most caring person I'd ever met.

Normally when I thought about her, I cried. Still. After all these years. But not today.

I hadn't cried since the day of Ned's visit. Maybe if he hadn't come, I'd have thought of last Wednesday as *the day that Carey left.* But the enormity of Ned's news trumped the official demise of a relationship that was over months ago.

Before Ned had knocked on my door, I'd been wondering about the next chapter in my life. The Carey-less chapter. I'd worried. I didn't know what it would look like.

Now, this next chapter was *the meeting Piper chapter.*

I wondered if it would be a short chapter or a long one.

I hoped it would be a good one. No matter what I found in Piper George, I hoped that as this chapter came to a close, she'd be well again.

My family doctor had talked to Piper's doctor and then had arranged my test in Port Clinton. All that was left was to wait for the results. Between my doctor and the Internet, I'd learned that the best chance of a bone marrow match came from siblings. Child to parent or parent to child matches weren't nearly as common. According to my doctor, I was a long shot. I tried to remind myself that my dad was right—a long shot was better than no shot.

I-90 snaked east from Port Clinton toward Erie. After I went through Cleveland, the traffic thinned.

I tried to stop worrying and concentrate on the fall beauty that was very much a part of the lakeshore. The trees that bordered the interstate here were brilliant reds, oranges, and yellows. Every now and then a V of geese flew into view through my car's windshield and then disappeared toward the south. On the ground, a group of geese is called a gaggle, but in the air it's known as a skein.

I liked that.

Different names for different perspectives.

The clouds were those puffy white autumnal clouds that spoke of cool days and the winter to come.

Most days this kind of beauty could distract me from almost any worry, but not today. My stomach was in knots.

I turned on the radio, but I found stations fading in and out of range annoying so tried my iPod. I put it on shuffle mode, but I couldn't make myself sing along. I was simply too anxious about my arrival in Erie. I had no idea what I would find.

I wasn't accustomed to going into a situation blind, and I found very little to recommend the experience. Maybe that's why I'd put off finding my birth mother. I wasn't good at diving into the unknown. As a programmer, I was used to concrete parameters: if X then Y; if Y then Z.

I'd told my business partner, Jaylin, that I was officially on vacation for a few weeks. We had no pressing projects, and she'd readily agreed.

When she asked why, I used the breakup with Carey as an excuse. I hadn't told Jaylin about Ned's visit or Piper or Piper being sick. I knew I would eventually, but everything was happening too fast for me to process, much less share the details with anyone other than Dad.

My thoughts and emotions went round and round as I made the less than three-hour drive. Ned's exit was just a mile away a sign proclaimed.

Despite the butterflies in my stomach, I felt a weird calm.

As I turned off the exit, my thoughts and emotions simply stopped, and all that was left was a feeling of flatness.

Ned had offered to let me stay in the house he'd lived in before he'd married Piper. After, he'd moved in with her, they'd kept his for others to use whenever there was a need.

I wanted to ask what kind of need, but I didn't. I wanted to ask who kept a house and then just loaned it out to other people, but I didn't ask that, either.

Our two conversations on the phone had been short and perfunctory. I didn't know what to say to him, and I don't think he knew what to say to me.

Ned said I was welcome to stay at his house for the night or for as long as I wanted to stay. He was leaving the key under the doormat for me.

I thought his offer showed a great deal of empathy. Staying at his house would allow me to be close to my biological mother without being, well, too close.

My GPS told me to take the next exit and informed me the road I was turning on to was Peach Street.

It was a busy road. Stores and restaurants lined the street. Some of the names I recognized; some I didn't. Jaylin would be squealing with glee at the sight of so many shopping opportunities. Me? I preferred shopping online. It seemed so much easier.

Need something? In just a couple of clicks, it was on its way to your front door.

I drove down Peach Street until the GPS had me turn right on to Thirty-Eighth Street. There were a few businesses and then a sign for the Erie Zoo. The street became busier but more residential. There were a few nonresidential businesses, a VA Hospital, and then Mercyhurst University. Finally, I turned into a residential neighborhood.

Piper George might be a bestselling author, but she wasn't playing lady of the manor. This was a very middle class neighborhood.

After I'd read the older Piper George books I owned, I'd looked her up on the Internet. She'd done a lot of writing in the last decade. Books I'd never read. Given all her books, I'd expected some kind of gated community or at least a suburban McMansion.

The neighborhood I found myself driving in wasn't either of those things. I pulled on to a quiet street. On the south side was a huge, sprawling school with the standard playground next to it. I watched the house numbers on the north side of the street. The GPS alerted me that I had arrived, and I finally pulled up in front of the number Ned had given me. It was a small brick home with a flair of Tudor styling at the peak. Those wooden beams sort of framed it all in. It had a family feel.

I could have pulled in the driveway, but I didn't want to announce that I'd arrived. I wanted a moment or two to collect myself before I went over to meet my birth mother.

I got out of the car and looked at her house.

Piper George's house.

My biological mother's house.

It was brick as well but more of a Cape Cod style. It had a large front porch that ran along the entire front of the house.

21

I could walk across the small yard and up on that porch. I could just knock and meet the woman I'd spent my life wondering about.

I could, but I didn't.

Instead, I grabbed my small suitcase and went to Ned's old house and let myself in with the key he had indeed left under the mat.

The interior was spartan but serviceable. There was a couch, a recliner, and a big television in the living room. I went to the back of the house and found a small but functional kitchen.

I'd told Ned I was coming today, but he hadn't asked me about a time so there were no expectations on his part. Even though I'd parked on the street, I was pretty sure he'd see the Ohio license plate on my car and know it was me.

He said he wouldn't say anything to Piper until I was ready. And I wasn't ready yet.

I walked into the dining room. I could see Piper's house through the windows. And over a solid wooden fence, I could make out a lot of fading fall greenery spiced up by punctuations of autumnal colors in her backyard.

Curious, I went upstairs to get a better look.

I walked into the closest back bedroom, sure that I'd have a better vantage point. I dropped my suitcase on the floor and found a barely clothed man sprawled out on the bed sleeping. Whether he was sleeping soundly or had simply closed his eyes I couldn't be sure because the moment I spotted him I said, "Oh," and turned to leave.

But not before noticing that the boxers he wore were black and covered with little yellow smiley faces.

"Hey, wait," Mr. Naked Smiley Face called.

I rushed out of the room, slamming the door behind me. "I'm so sorry. Ned said no one would be here."

I realized I had left my suitcase in the room, but I didn't go back for it. I mean, I could replace everything in it with one quick Internet shopping trip. I could even break down and go to a store. So I simply hurried down the stairs. I heard the door upstairs open and then footsteps following me down the stairs.

I was relieved to see that the seminaked man had pulled on some shorts and was sliding a T-shirt over his head as he approached me, his bare feet slapping each tread.

He was tan, whether by genetics or from the sun I wasn't sure. He had light brown hair, and as he reached the bottom of the staircase, I realized he was only a couple of inches taller than me.

"I'm so sorry," I said again.

He blinked his very blue eyes and then nodded.

I hadn't been able to sort out my emotions since the day Ned showed up on my porch. But I could identify this emotion. Embarrassment. And maybe a stirring of another feeling, but I planned to ignore that one.

"Ned said no one was using the house right now when he said I could stay here," I said in a rush, anxious to be on my way. I wasn't sure where I was going to go, but I knew it would be someplace other than here.

"I just got in last night at about three in the morning. Ms. Pip said to use my key. She said to use the house as long as I wanted. I'd have stayed with Mom, but she's moved out to Girard and I'm going back to school here in Erie. I have a year of my graduate degree done, so I've only got one more to go. I'm going to look for an apartment but . . ." His lengthy explanation faded. "Ms. Pip said no one else was using the place."

"Looks like their wires got crossed. Well, not really crossed. Piper doesn't know that I'm here," I confessed. Ned had called her Pip. This man called her Ms. Pip. Neither name felt right to me, though I didn't know what to call her.

The man raised his eyebrow, his question evident.

"I am heading over there in a minute. I came here first because . . ." Because I was stalling. That's why. But I didn't owe that explanation to this man.

"I'm Logan, by the way. Logan Greer. I feel as if women who've seen me in my boxer shorts should know my name."

It was a joke. I tried to smile but wasn't sure I'd managed a convincing one. "Siobhan. Siobhan Ahearn."

"How do you know Ned?" he asked.

I shook my head. "I don't really."

"Ms. Pip?" he asked.

I shook my head. "I don't know either of them really."

He raked his fingers through his sleep-tousled hair. "I don't think I understand. I'm still jet-lagged, so I'm a bit slower than normal."

"I don't know you well enough to explain." The words came out more snarky than I'd intended, and I saw that he'd taken offense.

"Okay then," he said slowly.

"I'll just get my stuff and leave," I said.

This meeting would give me the excuse I needed to go. I could put off meeting Piper a little longer if I had to go find a hotel.

"No. I mean, if you need to go see them, go. We'll figure out the house after you're done. I can always find a couch to crash on. To be honest, I can crash with Mom until I find a place. It just seemed a bit emasculating to have to live with my mom at my age."

I found myself trying to guess his age. Late twenties? Early thirties? I wasn't sure, but I knew it didn't matter.

"I . . ."

I started to say no, it was fine, I'd just leave, but I was afraid if I took my bag back to the car, I'd get in and just turn around and head back to Ohio.

I don't know that I could make anyone else understand how torn I was. I'd wanted to meet my biological mother for a long time. Yet here I was, and I was hesitating. It didn't make sense to me, so I was sure it wouldn't make sense to anyone else. I didn't say any of this to Logan. I just nodded, agreeing.

"If you were going upstairs to freshen up, you're welcome to. The bathroom's the door next to the room I was in. The middle door at the back of the house."

"Actually, I was going to see if I could get a look at Ned and Piper's backyard from your room's window. It looks like a jungle from over the fence, and I thought the upstairs window would have a better view," I confessed.

"Oh, Ms. Pip's not-so-secret garden. You need to see it in person to get the full feel of it. My mom likes it in the spring. She says there's a sense of possibility in a spring garden. I actually like it better now. So many of Ms. Pip's trees and plants change colors, it's amazing. Come on."

I knew that going upstairs with a strange man wasn't wise, but I didn't feel any sense of danger emanating from Logan Greer. To be honest, it was hard to be nervous about a man if you knew he was wearing smiley face boxers under his shorts.

So I followed him as he padded back up the staircase, his bare feet slapping on each tread. He led me back into the room and to the window.

"There," he said, pointing.

From this window, I could see over the fence and into the backyard. It was a sea of color. Some of the branches had lost enough of their leaves that we could see through them. The ground below the trees was green fading to brown. There were pops of reds, oranges, and golds. I could barely make out the path that wove through the yard to the picnic table at the front next to the house.

There was a fence that separated Piper's yard from Ned's, but the entire center section of the fence was missing. I could catch the edge of more fall-fading greenery spilling into the yard behind this house.

Logan answered my unasked question about it. "When Ms. Pip and Ned got married and decided to keep this place, she started expanding her garden into his yard." He pointed toward the back corner. "You should hear them every spring. She goes to the nursery, and he tells her she can't possibly fit one more plant in either yard. She ignores him, and when they get home, he's right there, helping her squeeze them in."

He pointed to a tree in Ned's back corner. "I helped plant that chestnut tree. It's a Chinese chestnut. The American ones got some disease and died off so most, if not all, that are left here aren't the native ones."

It was a fair-sized little tree, so I asked, "You've known them a long time?"

I was more anxious to hear about Ned and Piper than chestnuts.

"I've known them since I was a kid," he said.

"How did you meet them?" I asked.

Logan looked at me and said, "I'll tell you how I met Ms. Pip if you're really interested. But at this moment, I don't think you really want to hear my story."

"I don't?" I found it cheeky that this man presumed to know me well enough to know what I wanted or didn't want.

"You're stalling," he said simply.

"I beg your pardon?" I asked sharply.

Rather than look rueful, he laughed. He stopped short as he looked at me. I figured my frown was daunting, but he ruined that assumption when he grinned and said, "You sounded like my grandmother. *I beg your pardon?*" He laughed again.

"I . . ." I didn't know what to say to that, and that one syllable was as far as I went.

"I'm not sure why Ned brought you here without Ms. Pip knowing, but I'm pretty sure it wasn't to hear about how I met them. You're wound up tight over it, though. If you really need to stall, I'll tell you how I met her now, or we can do it later. Or you can tell me why you're meeting her."

"Why would I tell that to a stranger?"

"Sometimes it's easier to talk to someone who doesn't know you." He shrugged. "Either way, I'll be around."

He led me back down the stairs and walked me to the front door.

I don't want to say that Logan pushed me out, but he made it apparent that he wasn't going to aid my stalling.

"Don't forget, you're welcome to stay. There are extra bedrooms, and Ms. Pip will vouch for my character," were his parting words before he shut the door on me.

I looked across the driveway at Piper's porch.

Then slowly, I walked across the drive and to the porch. On one side of the door were comfortable-looking wicker chairs. They had red-and-blue plaid cushions and a small table sat between them. A plant and a teacup with small purple flowers sat on it. On the other side of the porch was a swing. It faced Ned's old house.

The only thing that separated me from the house proper was a screen door. Just one thin bit of screening between me and the woman who'd given birth to me and then had given me to my parents.

I stood absorbing the fact that Piper George lived here, in this very normal-looking house in the middle of a normal middle class neighborhood, only three hours away from where I lived.

I raised my hand to knock, but then I let it fall back to my side. I wasn't ready. Though I wasn't sure how anyone could be

27

ready for a situation like this. Maybe I'd just go back next door and get Logan to tell me how he'd met Piper and Ned.

Maybe I'd just get back in my car and—

A woman with a robin's-egg blue scarf tied over her hair came to the door. She looked pale and thin. Unnaturally thin. It was the type of thinness that didn't speak of diets or nature, but rather it spoke of illness.

No, not spoke—shouted.

I'd looked up Piper George's picture on the Internet. This was not how she'd looked. She'd had red hair, like mine. And she'd had an inviting smile. The type of smile that said, you can tell me your secrets and your hopes. You can tell me your dreams and your goals.

She smiled now, and despite the difference between that photo and the woman standing in front of me, that smile was still the same.

"Hi. Can I help you?" she asked.

"I—" That's all the further I got before I saw the first hint of recognition in her face. I answered her unasked question. "I'm Amanda."

I should have introduced myself as Siobhan Ahearn. But I knew that for her—for Piper—I'd always been Amanda. That one snippet from her journal and Ned's letter said as much. But even without that, I'd have known as I read her dedications in book after book.

I saw the tears form in her eyes, but she didn't cry. Instead, she shot me a smile and said, "Of course you are."

She opened the screen door and stepped out onto the porch next to me. "I've been waiting for you," she said softly.

"I know," I told her.

She reached out and touched my cheek as if she needed to be sure I was real. "*We've* been waiting for you."

I knew she meant her and Ned.

"Come in," she said.

I suddenly felt as if I couldn't breathe. I was afraid it would be worse inside, so I asked, "Could we go sit in your garden?"

I'm not sure why I wanted to go there so badly, but Piper didn't seem to mind.

"Of course."

She led me off the porch and along the side of the house to a gate that opened into the garden. It had looked amazing from the window of Ned's house, but that hadn't come close to doing it justice.

Patches of fall flowers dotted the ground. Some I recognized. Mums and some sort of daisy. But some I didn't. There was a low plant covered in purple flowers and some tiny white flowers. A bush with bright red berries. And surrounding those islands of color, it was green. Green leaves on the trees and the bushes as well as the ground cover. It was a tired green that spoke of the end of the season. Some of it had already morphed into browns, oranges, and reds. Some would never change color but would simply give up and fall to the already leaf-ridden ground.

"It's like the fairy garden in *Jenny Jangle and the Frisco Kid*," I whispered. "It looked amazing from upstairs, but up close—"

Piper interrupted. "Upstairs?"

I realized I'd thrown Ned under the proverbial bus.

"When were you in my house?" she asked.

"Never," I confessed. "I saw the garden from Ned's house."

"Ned's house?" she repeated, though she punctuated those two words with a question mark that said Ned was definitely going to hear about this.

I pointed to the back window. "I'm staying there. Well, I was, but your friend Logan's there, so I don't know where I'm staying. He said we'd figure it out after I came to meet you."

"I'm confused," she said. More than confused, she looked as if a stiff breeze would topple her over.

"Do you mind if we sit down?" I asked. "I'm so nervous I can't believe my knees aren't knocking."

"I'm so sorry," she said. "Of course."

She led me to an iron bench at the back of the garden. There was a patch of spikes with large leaves that had tumbled to the ground and what looked to be drying seedpods next to it.

"What's that?" I asked, not because of any driving need to know what that patch of plants was, but more because I wasn't sure what to say to this woman who was a stranger and yet was so much more.

"Milkweed. Monarch caterpillars eat it." She looked at me for a long minute, studying me. "So, you've met Ned and Logan?"

I ignored the Ned part because I wasn't sure what to say. Instead I zeroed in on the Logan part. "I'm pretty sure meeting Logan counts as a memorable meeting. I walked in on him, half-naked and asleep. Did you know he wears smiley face boxers?"

She laughed. "Yes, that's memorable. And no I didn't. But how did you come to be at Ned's?"

I didn't know how to answer her. Ned must have known she'd find out he'd found me, but I still felt as if I were betraying a confidence. In the end, I didn't need to say anything.

"He came and told you?" she asked, but we both knew it was more of a statement.

I nodded. "Yes. But to be fair, I could have been tested at home and simply let you think I was an anonymous donor if I were a match," I said. "I wanted to meet you."

I could see the doubt in her eyes. "You've had years and never made the move."

"It's complicated." As I said the words, I suddenly realized the source of my conflict, because even now, sitting with Piper, I felt

30

guilty. Even with my father's blessing I felt as if I were somehow betraying my mother.

I'm not sure exactly when I'd realized that was a big part of the reason I hadn't gone looking for my birth mother, but it was a big part of it.

The biggest part of it.

I knew it wasn't rational. Before she'd died, Mom and I had talked about my adoption. My hand touched my collarbone and felt the locket that I wore. My mother had given it to me along with the letter from my birth mother—from Piper. Mom had encouraged me to find her. Despite knowing all that, there it was. Guilt.

Piper didn't press. She simply nodded. "This isn't how I dreamed we'd meet."

"How did you dream it?" I asked. There were so many things I wanted to ask her, and I was sure she had things she wanted to ask me. But here we sat on a garden bench, two strangers looking for something benign to talk about because the heavier topics might crush us under their weight of emotion.

"I've dreamed meeting you so many times. I'd be sitting on the porch with Ned. We'd be talking about our day and then a car would pull up in front of the house. You'd get out, and I'd recognize you immediately. We wouldn't say anything because we couldn't. We'd be crying too hard for words. But we'd hug each other. I'd finally hold you again after so many years apart. The missing piece of my heart would finally be back where it belonged."

And that's all it took.

I was crying, and she was crying. And we hugged. We hugged for the longest time, this mother I'd never met but who'd loved me every minute of my entire life.

"Amanda," she whispered.

And she was right, some missing piece—a piece I'd never known was missing—was back where it belonged.

When the tears slowed, we both reluctantly let the other go. "It wasn't your front porch, but I hope it came close."

She took my hand in hers and patted it. "You're here just as I always dreamed."

"I have questions. So many questions that I don't know where to start."

She smiled. "Me, too. I guess the one that has haunted me the most is are you happy? Did you have a good childhood? Are you happy now?"

"My childhood—that one's easy. Yes. My parents were the best." I realized that might hurt her and started to look for something else to say. She must have sensed it, because she reached out and placed her hand on mine.

"That was my biggest dream for you. If you had a happy childhood, then, at least for me, most of the rest is secondary. Are you happy now? I—"

Piper was interrupted by someone hollering from the back door of the house. "Where are you?"

"Back here, Fi," she called.

Moments later, someone crashed into view. The someone in question was a young girl with a long braid that she flipped over her shoulder as she reached us.

A long red braid.

"Mom." She started and then noticed me.

She screeched and threw herself at me. I had no choice but to open my arms and catch her. "You're here, Amanda," she said as she hugged me.

"Her name's Siobhan," Piper said.

The girl released me and grinned at me. "Yeah, I know you're really Siobhan. I've seen the video about a thousand times. We watch it every year on your birthday. I can recite your whole speech by heart, you know."

She stood in front of me and recited:

There are so many choices. And each one we make will have a lifelong impact. I know about that kind of life-changing decision. You see, today I need to thank both of my mothers for the choices they made. I thank the mother who raised me. She opened her heart and her home to a child she didn't give birth to. That decision—made before I was born—set my life on a path. Never has any child been so loved.

But I also need to thank the mother who gave birth to me. Most of you don't know I'm adopted. Why would you? But before I was my parents' daughter, there was another woman who carried me for nine months.

"Fiona," Piper said sharply, warning in her voice.

It took me a moment, but I recognized the speech from my high school graduation. I'd been valedictorian. My parents had given me the letter from my birth mother and the locket. I reached up and touched it as if it were a talisman that might calm me.

"Video?" I asked. I was struck by the enormity of this girl's appearance. I had a sister. A sister who knew my entire valedictorian speech from high school.

"Oh, sorry, Mom." She turned back to me. "I'm Fiona. Mom and Dad loved your name so much—Siobhan," she added, as if I might not be sure what name she was talking about. "So when I came along, they decided on an Irish name for me, too. Of course, they didn't really think too much about the impact of a name like Fiona. Some of the bullies at school tried to taunt me by calling me Shrek, but then I said if I were

33

an ogre, they must be the donkey, only I called them another word that means donkey and the teacher overheard. She called Mom and Dad in along with Dillan's parents. We had to apologize to each other. He tried calling me Shrek again, but I just brayed at him like a donkey, and then I said I couldn't understand donkey. He gave up."

"Fi—" Piper said.

"That's Mom's way of saying I talk too much, and I do. But I've got a lot to say to you. I'm nine, and I've been waiting for you my whole life. You can't imagine how hard it was to be patient. Mom says that patience isn't one of my virtues."

"Neither is silence," Piper said, dire warning in her voice.

If my mother had spoken to me in that tone, I'd have been cowed. My little sister was either made of sterner stuff, or Piper was less than intimidating because Fiona simply grinned and said, "Yeah, silence isn't one, either."

"Honey, Siobhan just got here, and we'd like some time to talk."

"Okay, I get it. But you have to promise me you won't just leave without seeing me." She reached out and hugged me again. "Promise."

I nodded. "I promise."

"Okay. Should I call Grandma and tell her?" Fiona asked Piper.

Piper shook her head. The tails of her scarf fell over her shoulder, where her hair should have been, reminding me that she was very ill.

"No. Not yet," Piper told Fiona.

I had a grandmother who was still alive. I wondered what other family Piper—I—had.

"Gotcha." Fiona turned as if she was going to run back into the house, but in the end she turned around and hugged me one more time. "I've waited for you my whole life, and I can wait a little longer."

She turned and ran back toward the house, and as she disappeared into Piper's garden I heard her call, "But not too much longer."

"I have a sister," I said out loud.

"Yes."

"The video?" I asked.

She sighed. "I didn't tell Ned about you for a long time. I didn't tell anyone. Not because I was embarrassed that I'd been a teen mom," she added quickly, "but because I had so little of you that I hoarded the memory and moments. I clung to them and kept them to myself."

She shrugged. "I don't know how to explain it better than that. When I finally told Ned, he went to find you. Not to interrupt your life, but to let me know you were okay. He realized that everything I'd done was part of my worry for you. I worried that you were hungry or hurting. That you needed me and I wasn't there. He just went to check, and you were graduating so he attended the ceremony and filmed your graduation and speech." She got choked up and stopped. Finally she whispered, "It was the most amazing gift anyone's ever given me."

I remembered. And I reached to my neck and again touched the locket I'd worn since Ned's visit.

"I talked about you," I said.

She nodded. "And you wore the locket."

I pulled it into view now.

"Seeing you," she said and then stopped and took a deep breath. "Hearing that you were okay and that you didn't blame me but thanked me instead, it made all the difference. I'd never thought I'd have other children because I worried that someday you'd find me and you'd be hurt if you discovered that after giving you away I had children that I kept, but you said . . ."

I nodded. I'd said that when I found my birth mother, I hoped she had a large family. "I meant it. I'm so glad you had Fiona."

I felt awkward again. "I don't know what to say, what to ask."

"Are you involved with anyone?" she asked, giving me some direction.

"I was. For a very long time. But the day Ned came, I was in the process of throwing him out of the house. I've decided to take a break from men for a while."

"Did he do something wrong, or did you simply outgrow each other?"

She didn't ask if I'd done something wrong. My father and Margo—my stepmother—hadn't, either, when I told them. They'd wanted to know what Carey had done.

"He cheated," I admitted. I hadn't told anyone else that. I'd just said we'd grown apart. The fact he'd cheated was embarrassing. I didn't want to continue this line of discussion, so I said, "Will you tell me about your illness?"

She looked disappointed.

"Was that the wrong thing to ask?" I asked.

She shook her head. "It simply sometimes feels as if I've disappeared and all that's left is my cancer. It eats up so much of my life. I've stepped down from volunteering, and I haven't been able to write. It's the first time since I wrote my first Belinda Mae story that I can't write. And I resent the hell out of that. You know the first thing anyone asks me now is 'how are you?' I know they're being kind and that they're concerned, but they don't really mean *how are you*; what they mean is *how is your cancer*. I am more than my disease."

"I'm sorry, I—"

She shook her head. "No. Don't be. That was just ridiculous and uncalled for. Of course you want to know. You're here to help me."

"I'm here to meet you and to help you if I can."

And if I couldn't help? What if this was it? My only chance to know Piper? What if I couldn't help her, and I lost her just after I found her?

I'd wasted years staying away because of some unnecessary guilt.

"I have leukemia." She talked in the technical terms of someone who'd lived with a disease far too long. She defined it and then talked about the symptoms. She talked about chemo. She talked about losing her appetite for not only food but her work as well. "I've gone into remission before and thought each time that it would last, but it never lasts. And the treatments are . . ."

She shook her head. "If it hadn't been for Ned and Fiona, and for the possibility of meeting you, I might have stopped fighting." She gave herself a tiny shake. Just a twitch of her head and shoulders. "Don't tell Ned and Fi I said that, please."

"I won't," I promised.

"They found the cancer when Fi was four. I've been fighting it more than half her life. She doesn't remember a time when her mother was well. Oh, there have been those remissions, but they're just a tease. They just show her what we could have but don't."

"And a bone marrow transplant would cure you?"

"That's what they hope. There could be complications from the transplant, too, so in the end it's all a crap shoot."

"I've done some reading and it seems that I'm a long shot."

"That's why I didn't actively pursue it. I couldn't see interrupting your life for a pipe dream. I didn't want you to come meet me out of pity—"

"Pity? That's not what this is. My mom and dad never hid the fact I was adopted, but they didn't share your letter until I was older. They gave it to me along with the locket." I fingered it as I so often did. "I thought about finding you. I planned on it. Then my mother got sick and . . ."

"Life happened," she said.

I wasn't ready to talk about my mother with Piper so I just nodded. "I'm glad Ned came. Finding you, wanting to know you, that's not pity. I hope I can help you, but no matter what, I want an opportunity to know you. To know Ned and Fiona, too."

She sat for a moment as if digesting that and then asked, "How long can you stay? I imagine you only have so long from work. Where do you work? Where do you live? I . . ." She laughed. "I could ask you questions all night—for weeks or even months—and never feel as if I knew enough. I promise, I'll try to behave."

I understood what she was saying. With most people finding out about them in bits and dribbles was fine, but with Piper, I wanted to know it all right now.

"I'm self-employed," I told her. "My friend Jaylin and I have a business. We make apps for, well, lots of things. Companies hire us, and we tailor our designs around their needs or products. It's not very exciting, well it is for us but not for most other people. On the plus side, I can work from anywhere. Ned said I could stay at his house, and I planned to, but now Logan's there."

For a moment, I was afraid she'd ask me to stay with them. I wanted to know them, but that would be too overwhelming.

"I'd say you're welcome to stay with us, but that would be too much for you," she said as if she could read my mind. "I'm sure Logan wouldn't mind a roommate. Between work and then graduate classes, he'll be gone more than he's there."

"He said as much."

"It's the truth. He's one of the hardest-working men I've ever known. But he's more than hard work. He's compassionate. Even as a little boy. When my dog died, I was beyond upset. I know it sounds crazy, but I loved Bruce. He was older when I adopted him, and I had warnings that he wouldn't last much longer, but when the time finally came, I was distraught. Logan helped Ned bury him in the garden. A few weeks later, he brought me a marker as a present. Logan understood how devastated I was. His kindness helped me. If you get up and look behind the milkweed, right next to the fence, you'll see it."

I did, and there was a small brass marker. "Bruce. He was a good dog and a good friend," I read aloud. Next to it was a similar marker. "Princess. She's finally home with Bruce."

"Ned and I adopted them before we were married. I watched Princess whenever he traveled, and after we married, the dogs were inseparable. Princess loved us, but she simply couldn't go on without Bruce."

She wiped at her eyes and then added, "Between you and me, I think part of the reason he came home to finish his last year of school was to keep an eye on me."

If she had looked as if a stiff wind would blow her over when I'd first shown up at her door, she looked as if a soft sneeze could do as much now.

"Piper, how sick are you?" I asked.

"Sick enough," she said vaguely.

"Maybe sick enough that this is overwhelming and you should lie down for a while?" I asked softly.

"I don't want to miss out on—"

She looked pale, and I saw a light sheen of sweat on her brow.

"I'm not going anywhere. Not for a while. We'll have time, I promise. Why don't you go lie down and rest for a bit, and I'll go talk to Logan and get settled in. I'll come back later."

She gripped my hand. "Promise?"

"I promise." I stood and helped her up and then held her arm as we walked back through the tangle of plants and trees.

"Come back for dinner," she said. "At five."

"I will," I promised.

"I've been waiting your whole life to meet you," she said softly.

39

"I'm here, and I'm not going anywhere anytime soon," I promised her again.

I took Piper to her back door and promised to come over for dinner later. Then I walked back into the garden and through the hole in the fence that led to Ned's backyard. I could see what Logan had meant. It was as if Piper's garden was slowly spilling into his yard.

There was a small patch of grass on the far end, but here, near the fence, there was a row of bushes that came up to my knee. Old leaves were breaking, scattered at its base. Little patches of smaller plants grew around trees. Two of the trees weren't much bigger than me—I couldn't tell what kind they were.

I went into the corner, to Logan's chestnut tree, and then I leaned back against the fence post and thought that maybe I should cry, but I couldn't. So many emotions roiled inside me. I was happy I'd met her. Sad she was sick. Worried that I wouldn't be a match. Curious to know more. Heartsick knowing she'd grieved over losing me. Surprised that I had a sister. I was . . .

There were just too many emotions swirling and tumbling one over another. I couldn't pin any of them down. I couldn't hold on to one of them long enough to truly feel it. I gave up and headed toward the house to talk to Logan and see if he really meant it was okay for me to stay there.

I knocked on the door, and he opened it moments later. He was still fully clothed. He looked at me and nodded, seemingly confirming something to himself.

"I talked to Piper and—"

"You're Amanda?" It sounded like a question, but I could see in his eyes that he knew.

"How—" I started to ask.

"Fiona," he quickly added as he ushered me inside. "You looked familiar, and I should have had it when you said your name, but you've always simply been Amanda to me."

"Piper said she hadn't told anyone about me. When she finally did, Ned checked on me."

"Ms. Pip didn't talk about you even as she built a life around you." Logan spoke as if he understood. I thought about what Piper had said about his empathy when she lost her dog. I suspected she was right.

"If she didn't talk about me—"

"Fiona," he said, answering my incomplete question. "Fi celebrates your birthday for you every year. Years ago, I was home between trips and she invited me, Cooper, and her grandparents to the party. Finding out about you explained so many things about Ms. Pip. Fi's been waiting for you. I think she thought that someday you'd show up on your birthday. It's always an event. She sends me pictures if I'm overseas. She makes a cake and decorates. But you never came."

I could hear him wondering why I'd come now. "Ned found me and told me that Piper was sick. My doctor ran tests at home to see if I'm a match, but I don't have the results yet."

"Is her illness the only reason you came?"

I realized that I didn't owe this man—this stranger—any more of my story. As we stood in the center of Ned's kitchen, I realized the idea of staying didn't seem wise. "I should be going."

"Don't. If either of us should go anywhere, it should be me. But I meant what I said; I'll hardly ever be here. Between work and school you'll hardly know I'm here."

I thought about arguing, but he continued.

"There are three bedrooms upstairs. You obviously know where mine is. Pick one of the other ones and settle in. I promise I won't pepper you with personal questions, despite the evidence to the contrary."

He shot me a wry grin. It was scampish. It was the kind of grin that said he was probably one of those kids who was always

41

in trouble in school. Not detention or suspension sort of trouble, but rather the kind of kid whose name the teacher used—a lot.

I knew I should go, but I didn't want to. I wanted a chance to know Piper. Even if I weren't a match, I wanted to be here, close to her. "Are you sure?"

He nodded. "To be honest, when I was overseas I shared a room with four other volunteers. We slept in shifts. Having a whole room to myself seems decadent. Having the entire house seems lonely."

"All right. Thank you." I walked toward the stairs and then stopped. "Would you tell me how you met Piper?"

"Are you still stalling?" he asked with a smile that told me he was teasing.

I shook my head. "I think I wore her out, so I sent her in to rest. She invited me back for dinner. So, no, I'm not stalling."

Logan nodded and we both walked into the living room. "You know she's a writer?"

"I grew up reading her books, though I didn't know she was my birth mother then." I sat on the far end of the couch. "After Ned came, I dug them all out of the attic and reread all the ones I had. I know she's written a lot since then. I plan on catching up."

"Do you know about the rest?" he asked.

"Rest?"

"Have you read her bio or any of the articles on her?"

I shook my head. "I looked her up on the Internet. I realized she'd written a lot of books, and I found her picture." I didn't add that she didn't look like that picture now.

"Ms. Pip started and ran a food pantry—Amanda's Pantry. Over the years, she expanded it and added Amanda's Closet, supplying winter coats to the kids who visited, and Amanda's Bookshelf, giving them free books. But more than all that, she cared. She helped. After she married Ned, they kept his house and used it over the years to help out families. Mine was one of those."

"Pardon?" I asked.

He smiled as I said the word, and though we'd just met, I could read his teasing in just his expression.

"My mom got pregnant when she was in high school and dropped out of school before she graduated," he said. "We used Amanda's Pantry. But you have to understand that Ms. Pip didn't just hand out food. She talked to the people. She got to know my mom. We were couch-surfing most of the time, and Mom worked at odd jobs here and there. Long story short, Ms. Pip offered us this house on the condition that Mom went back to school. So Mom got her GED and then trained as an electrician. Other people occasionally stayed with us for a while, but Mom and I were here through my last year of high school."

He paused a moment and then added, "It was the first time we ever had a consistent home. It was the first time I'd ever had a room to call my own. When Mom got a job, we got an apartment, and Ms. Pip had other families stay here."

I thought he was done, but Logan added softly, "Mom bought her own home a few years ago in Girard. Not just a place to rent, but *bought* it. I came home for the closing. Unless you knew where she'd come from, you might not understand how significant it was. The first thing she did once we moved her in was have a dinner for Ms. Pip, Ned, and Fi."

I could imagine it. A small house all lit up, and Ned and Piper being invited in. That sense of pride that Logan's mom must have felt.

I thought he was done, but then Logan added, "Because Ms. Pip changed my mom's life, she changed mine. It wasn't just having a house to call home or a room of my own. I went to college. And I became a nurse, like Ms. Pip."

"She's a nurse?" I asked. I'd read her bio online and had seen her picture, but I hadn't gone surfing for more in-depth information. Logan knew so much more about my biological mom than I did.

He nodded. "That's what she was doing when she became a writer. I'm going back to school to be a nurse practitioner. I finished the first year and then did another stint with First Aid, an international medical relief organization. I've already signed up to go abroad again next year when I've finished—"

He was interrupted by the sound of the front door banging open. Fiona raced into the room. "You're still here."

There were so many confusing emotions still tossing about in me, but when I looked at Fiona, things were clear. She was a kid I already genuinely liked. "Yes. I'm coming to dinner tonight, and Logan invited me to stay here."

"If you weren't staying here, I was going to tell you that you could stay at our house."

Her offer was earnest. "Thank you, Fiona."

"Maybe sometime we'll have a sleepover." I caught Logan grinning, and obviously so did Fiona. She glared at him. "I just met my sister for the first time. You can't blame me for being excited."

He pulled her braid. "No, I can't, squirt. But I'm guessing that this is very overwhelming for your sister."

I nodded. "I was an only child when I woke up this morning. My stepmom doesn't even have kids, so no stepsiblings," I admitted. "I'm not sure I know how to be a sister."

"Oh, it's easy. I've given it a lot of thought. You think that everything I do is wonderful, and if I'm fighting Mom and Dad over something, you're always on my side."

I couldn't help but grin. "Is that so?"

She nodded so hard her braid audibly thwacked against her back. "Yeah. I have plenty of friends with older siblings, so I know how it's supposed to go."

"I'll keep it in mind," I promised her.

"I'm actually here to see if you have anything you won't eat, or can't eat."

"Nope. No allergies or anything. And for won't—I'm pretty good with most normal foods."

"What's an abnormal food?"

"Things that have eyes and look at you while you eat them. Snails. Snakes . . ."

"Logan's eaten all kinds of creepy food, but I'm with you. So's Dad. He's not a great cook, but he's making spaghetti so we're pretty safe." She turned to Logan. "You're supposed to come over, too."

He shook his head. "This is for family."

"You're family," Fiona informed him.

"I know, but tonight I think it should be the four of you. I'll come over for dinner next time."

"Mom's not going to like your answer." She turned to me. "Everyone thinks Mom's so easygoing, but she has very firm opinions on things. Like finding you. Dad's going to be in the doghouse for a long time for this one."

"Why?" I asked.

"Because she didn't want to bother you. She didn't want to make you feel guilty, like you had to come. She wanted to wait for you to come on your own."

"But if I can help her?" I asked.

Fiona scoffed and sounded decades older than she was. "One of the first things you need to know about our mom is she'll help anyone she can, but she would never ask for help for herself."

Logan nodded his agreement.

"I'll see you at five. *Both of you,*" Fiona warned Logan, and then she scampered back out of the house as quickly as she had come.

45

"Fi's right. Ms. Piper would do whatever it took to help someone. But asking for help? She's not very good at that."

I suddenly didn't want to learn more about Piper George. A woman who'd given me up for adoption. A woman who was a nurse, a writer, an altruistic do-gooder, a mother, a wife. A woman who was battling cancer. A woman who knew I might be able to help but didn't want to *bother* me.

"I'm going to go get the rest of my stuff out of the car and then go upstairs until dinner, if you don't mind."

"I don't mind at all," he said.

I started to leave the room then Logan called, "Siobhan, you should call someone."

"Who?" I asked.

He shrugged. "I don't know. A family member, some friend. Just someone. This is a lot to take on. A lot to deal with."

I nodded, but I wasn't sure I was going to take his advice. I mean, how could I explain what was going on to someone else when I wasn't sure I could articulate it to myself? Meeting Piper and knowing she'd never forgotten me felt good. But meeting her and seeing her with Fiona made me miss my mother more than ever.

And though I knew it was crazy, it still made me feel guilty.

Chapter Three

"You can't judge a book by its cover," Belle told her mother.

"But you can judge a girl by her holey jeans. Go change,"
her mother insisted. Her mother wore an expression that brooked
no arguments.

It looked like Belle was going out to dinner, and her holey
jeans were not.

—Beautiful Belle, by Pip

I don't own many dresses—*any* dresses, to be honest. Most
of my business meetings are on Skype. All that's really
required for that is a halfway decent shirt and a scarf. I have half a
dozen scarves in a variety of colors. My style mantra is, you can't
go wrong with a scarf.

Jaylin does not share my casual dress style. When we were college roommates, she was forever trying to dress me up like some
doll. I normally balked at her attempts, but today I would give
anything if she were here in Erie instead of Asheville. She'd know
what to wear to a first meal with your biological mother.

Or what not to wear.

It seemed as if I had more *nots* than *possibilities* in my suitcases.

I'd brought one carry-on and one bigger suitcase with me. I
thought I had plenty of clothes to last me however long I stayed

in Erie. They were all casual. And I'd only packed one scarf. It was a black-and-brown patterned one. I hadn't really thought my packing through.

There was a knock on my door.

"Siobhan? Is everything okay?" Logan called.

"I don't have anything nice to wear."

Okay, that was a whine. I know it was a whine, but I couldn't help it. I was nervous. Piper had seemed nice enough. So had Ned and Fiona. Still, I couldn't shake the butterflies that were cartwheeling around in my stomach.

"Wear whatever you're comfortable in," Logan called through the door. "Ms. Pip won't care. I swear; she doesn't own jeans without holes in the knees."

I tried to remember what she had been wearing earlier. I couldn't. I remembered the scarf around her head—it was robin's-egg blue. And I remembered how gaunt her face looked, but I couldn't remember her clothes.

Thinking of Piper's scarf, I dropped my own back on the pile. I wasn't going to wear one tonight, I decided.

I looked down at my jeans. At least they didn't have holes in the knees, though my favorite pair in the pile of clothing on the bed did. And the white T-shirt and black cardie were dressy enough. I slipped my feet into my ballet flats and opened the door. "I want to make a good impression."

Logan was wearing jeans and a polo shirt. "They're not dressy people. And they're family. You'd look beautiful to them in Ms. Pip's holey jeans."

My accidental roommate was a very nice man. He nodded toward the stairs. "Are you ready?"

I nodded. "Thank you for coming with me. I know we've just met, but I feel like I have an ally."

"This isn't a battle, Siobhan. You don't need an ally, but maybe you need a friend. I can be that." He reached out and took my hand. It was simply for moral support—I got that. I took comfort in it as we walked across the driveway and up onto Piper's porch. I dropped his hand as I knocked.

"This is her office," he said conversationally, nodding at the chair on the porch. "Every year, as soon as the weather is even halfway warm enough, she's out here working every day. In the winter, she moves inside by the front window. I know that most people count robins as a true sign of spring, but everyone at school looked for Ms. Pip on the porch. That's how we marked the change of seasons."

"I work on my porch, too," I said.

In a world of nine-to-fivers, it was weird to find someone else who worked for themselves. Jaylin was the only other person I'd ever met who understood that sometimes having no boss was worse than working for a tyrant. I mean, when I got hung up on an encroaching deadline, I only had myself to blame.

I bet Piper would understand that.

It was a tangible connection to my birth mother that I hadn't considered before.

"Thanks," I told Logan just as Ned opened the door.

"Welcome home," Ned said as he threw the door open wide.

Logan and I stepped inside the house. Again, I was thankful for Logan's presence. He didn't wait for further invitation. He walked toward the back of the house—which I guessed was the kitchen—as if he'd done it hundreds of times.

He probably had.

But I hadn't. I stood, rooted to the spot, trying to catch my breath.

"It's overwhelming for Pip, too," Ned told me softly. "But I swear we don't bite."

Suddenly a giant hairy dog ran into the foyer and jumped at me. I had just enough time to brace myself before he hit me like a ton of bricks. There was no menace in him. He was tall enough that he began to lick my face, doing his part to assure me I was his new best friend.

Ned grabbed at his collar, but the dog wouldn't be denied. He wrestled to stay close to me.

"Killer watchdog?" I asked Ned, laughing as they battled.

He laughed. "Archie, down."

The dog thumped down to the floor, swinging his giant tail from side to side like some huge dust mop, seemingly not carrying that he was whacking it against the newel post.

I leaned down and patted his head, which made his tail wag even faster. "He seems sweet. What kind of dog is he?"

"A shepoodle," Ned answered. "At least that's what Fi calls him."

He looked like a dust mop. "I don't think I've ever heard of that."

"Part sheepdog, part standard poodle. I think there might be an official name for them, but Fi has firm opinions on everything," Ned supplied. He paused a moment as the dog flopped on to his back, telling me a stomach scratch was in order without saying a word. "He's obviously king of the castle."

Fiona came barreling into the living room so quickly she almost made Archie seem sedate. The dog jumped back up and ran over to kiss her and then came back to me.

"Mom said there's ten minutes till dinner, so you have time to come see my room before we eat," she blurted out in one breathless stream of words.

"Fiona, I don't think—" Ned started.

"It's okay. I'd love to see your room," I told her.

She took my hand, pulled me up the stairs as Ned called after us, "I'm going to help finish things up."

"I'll bring her down in a minute, Dad," Fiona called back to him.

She led me down a narrow hall to a bedroom door.

"My room," Fiona said, opening it with a flourish.

There was a huge stuffed horse in one corner, a dollhouse in another, bunk beds, and a dresser that looked as if a rainbow had exploded on it. Every available section of wall space was covered with bookshelves. "This is amazing."

I walked closer and noticed that the horse was wearing a cardboard horn. "Flo likes to disguise herself as a unicorn," Fiona said with a laugh. "When Mom's *Fi Fly Flo* hit its third month on the bestseller's list, her publisher sent her the horse."

"I didn't read that one. I reread all the ones I had, but I know she's written a lot since I outgrew them. I plan on buying them."

"Oh, don't do that," Fiona said with a laugh. "Mom gets author copies. She's got a ton in the attic. She gives them away for fundraising auctions all the time. Once she even let a fundraiser auction her off. Well, a date with her. It was a girl from Meadville who won. Mom took her out to lunch. Anyway, you don't have to buy 'em. She'll give you any of the new ones. I get copies of all of them." She led me to one of the shelves that was filled with Pip books. The other shelves were filled with books by a lot of authors I recognized. Zilpha Keatley Snyder. Madeleine L'Engle. C. S. Lewis. Laura Ingalls Wilder.

I picked up William McCleery's *Wolf Story*. "I've never met anyone else who read this. I loved it when I was a kid. My mom read it to me so many times."

"Mom read it to me, too. She loves books. She used to be the kindergarten story lady at the school across the street. She did it the year I was in kindergarten but stopped after that."

"Why did she stop?" I asked.

"Because she was sick," Fiona answered sadly.

What might that have been like? To grow up with a mother who was so sick? To have the specter of death always lurking in the background?

It was hard enough to walk into that situation for me as an adult, but for a little girl?

I reached out and patted Fiona's shoulder. What I really wanted to do was hug her and tell her everything would be all right, but I wasn't sure that was true.

"Dinner," Ned called from downstairs.

"I'm sorry," I said to Fiona. I didn't know what else to say to this girl who was my sister and yet also a stranger. I gave her shoulder another squeeze for good measure before she led me to the dining room.

Ned was putting serving plates on the table, and Piper was sitting next to Logan, listening to whatever he was saying, and smiling. But her smile seemed thin, like a veneer. As if she were physically forcing her lips into that upturned position. She was wearing a purple scarf over her head and looked even paler than she had that afternoon.

"Piper, are you okay?" I asked.

She turned that smile on me, and it was even more apparent that she was forcing it. "I'm fine. I'm just so glad you're here and that Logan's home."

"I was telling her about our introduction," Logan said in a chipper—too chipper—voice. "And assuring Ms. Pip that you are a much more preferable roommate than the last batch. One we called Pen. Short for Pigpen, which is exactly what he smelled like."

"Ew," Fiona said as she dropped into a chair across from Logan.

Piper patted the vacant chair next to her, and I obligingly sat down as well.

Logan didn't miss a beat. "Yeah, ew. I got a shower maybe once a week, but I washed. Water was scarce and hot water unheard of, but you could still wash. Pen claimed he couldn't stand the cold water. He also claimed he didn't smell. He was wrong. One day it had to have been over a hundred with ninety percent humidity.

The smell got so bad that we moved his bed into the yard while he slept—on it."

"Nuh-uh," Fiona said.

"Honest to Pete." Logan held up his fingers in a scouting sign. "We moved his mosquito netting, too, so it was all good. The house smelled so much better."

"How big a house was it?" Fiona asked.

"A bedroom-size house. There was enough room for two sets of bunk beds and Pen's single bed. There wasn't room for much else. We kept our clothes in the suitcases, which we stored under the bottom bunk."

Fiona and Logan saved the early part of the dinner. Every time his story wound down, the conversation ground to a halt until Fiona asked him another question and he wound back up again.

He was a natural storyteller. Some might think that it was the fact he'd traveled all over the world that gave him fodder for his tales, but as I listened, I would have to disagree. He had a way with words. He painted pictures out of his memories. Pictures that were so vivid it was easy to imagine being there.

Piper did more pushing of the pasta than eating it. I noticed her hand was trembling. I wasn't sure if it was me or her illness.

I reached over and patted her hand without thinking. She turned to me and smiled. She didn't turn her hand over and demand more from me. She simply accepted the comfort I was trying to give.

As Logan finished a story about his last trip, Piper asked me, "Have you traveled?"

"My parents were teachers. We went on vacations in the summer but not to Africa or South America like Logan. We went to national parks and historic cities. One year we rented a place on Prince Edward Island for a couple of weeks because I'd read L. M. Montgomery's books and wanted to see it."

"I've read all the *Anne* books," Fiona cried. "I figure with our hair, she's a *kindred spirit* for sure."

I nodded. "I think that's why I loved her so much. That was such a special vacation. I loved being on the beaches there. I imagined walking along with Diana and Gilbert. I recited poems as I walked along the water's edge."

"*The Lady of Shalott*," Piper and Fiona said together.

The three of us laughed while Ned and Logan looked confused.

"We'll have to take you to the peninsula while you're here," Piper said.

I didn't want to hurt her by talking about my parents, so I admitted I'd visit the peninsula but tried not to mention Mom and Dad. "I came here one year—to Erie. We rented a place at the mouth of the peninsula. I took pontoon boats through the lagoons and spent the days hiking and swimming."

"You were in Erie?" Piper asked shakily.

"Yes. And when I found out you were here, I . . ." I shrugged. I didn't know how to explain just how I felt. "We've always lived so close. Both of us on Lake Erie."

She smiled. "I find the thought comforting."

I patted her hand again, and she smiled. It looked more natural than her forced one. She had the kind of smile that looked as if it were her default expression—at least before she'd become so sick.

"I had Ned bring down your hope chest," she said. "It's in the living room. I'm sure Logan will carry it next door for you. I wrote you a notebook, or journal if you'd rather. And there are other things. Gifts I bought you. Some old family photos. I bought you a notebook, much like the one I wrote in for so many years. I thought that this experience—meeting me—might be hard on you, and I've always found writing a way of coping with my pain. The chest—" Her sentence ended abruptly as she jumped up and rushed out of the room.

"I'm sorry, I've got to help her," Ned said, racing after her.

"Food makes her sick," Fiona said. "Dad had to fight to help cook the spaghetti. I told her she didn't need to have a dinner for you. I told her that you'd understand, but Mom can be stubborn. She said that she'd fed hundreds and hundreds of kids in your name, the least she could do is have dinner with you, even if she wasn't up to cooking it."

I'm not sure why, but the thought of her having a dinner for me when food made her nauseous hit me. I could feel tears creeping to the edge of my eyes, but I blinked them back. "I should go."

"She's probably done for the night," Fiona said, sounding much older than nine. "But you'll be here tomorrow?"

"Yes," I said. "I'm in town for a while."

"Don't you have to work?" Fiona asked.

I shook my head. "I work for myself. I can work anywhere there's an Internet connection."

"Just like Mom. She works from home, too," Fiona said.

I didn't know what to say to that, but I didn't need to say anything. Fiona seemed capable of carrying on an entire conversation on her own. "I'll tell Mom to call you when she's ready for company. She'll want to see you as soon as she's able."

"Tell her that I'm not going anywhere."

"I will." Fiona hugged me. "I've waited for you my whole life."

I patted her back. I knew I was coming to meet Piper, and I'd been prepared for Ned, but Fiona had been a complete surprise.

She led us to the living room. "That's for you," she said, pointing at an obviously old wooden box. It had once been blue, but the paint was worn and faded, as were the red flowers that had been hand-painted on the front.

"It's been upstairs under Mom's bedroom window my whole life," Fiona said. "I always called Amanda's box. For years, she added a charm on your bracelet, and she's bought you some other little things, but it's the notebook that you'll want. I've never read it because it was for you. Just Mom and Dad have."

I started to reach for it, but Logan said, "Let me carry it for you," and he picked it up without waiting for me to respond.

I wanted to say no. I didn't want someone else touching this gift. But I nodded at him and turned to Fiona. "I'll see you tomorrow. Tell your mom and dad thank you for dinner."

"*Our* mom," she corrected. "And I will."

I didn't know how to explain to a nine-year-old that while I knew that Piper had given birth to me and I felt a connection, she could never be my mom. My mom had been Margaret Ahearn and my father was Patrick Ahearn. I would always be Pat and Maggie's daughter. I couldn't sort it all out, so I didn't respond. I just followed Logan across the driveway and back to Ned's old house.

I unlocked the door for him and followed him as he carried the box into the living room. "She's really sick."

"Yes," he said simply.

"If I'm not a match . . ."

"Then someone else will be," he said with far more assurance than I felt. "Ms. Pip's strong. She's fought her cancer for years because of Ned and Fiona. Now she's got you to fight for, too."

I nodded, but I wasn't sure I believed him. I walked to where he'd set the box down. I leaned over and touched it.

There were bare spots where the paint had given up completely, and in other places the blue had faded to almost gray. Small red flowers graced the front face of it. Time had changed them into a dusty rose, but it was easy enough to make out what they were.

The top, however, was more difficult. Decades of people putting things on top of the chest had hastened its aging. I could barely make out the letters T. P. E. and the numbers 1837 on the lid.

T. P. E.

I was no antique expert, but most of these boxes were for a woman's trousseau. T. P. E. would pack the chest with items she hoped she'd use in the marriage she dreamed about.

What had Piper put in mine? Were the items part of her hopes and dreams for me?

Logan cleared his throat, reminding me he was still there. "Do you want me to leave while you open it, or would you rather I carry it upstairs?"

I shook my head. "I don't think I can open it tonight."

"You don't have to," he said softly.

"It's only been a day. I thought I'd meet her and suddenly know just what to do about all this. How to feel about it all. Her being my birth mother and dedicating all those books to me, and now this." I pointed to the chest. "And her being sick and knowing how much Ned loves her."

Ned hadn't said much at dinner, but I could see his love for Piper every time he looked at her. "And a sister. I didn't expect that. I just don't know what to do, what to feel. I—"

"You don't have to sort it all out tonight," Logan said. "Listen, why don't you go upstairs and get some sleep. Tomorrow's another day."

"I need to call my dad first."

"I'll head up and leave you to it then. If you need anything, you know where my room's at." Logan said the words with a wicked grin and a quirking of his eyebrow.

Despite feeling utterly overwhelmed, I laughed, which I knew had been his intent.

"I've got to go to work a twelve-hour shift tomorrow. Seven at night to seven in the morning. I'll be around during the day if you need me. Afterward, make yourself at home. I didn't get to the grocery store, but you're welcome to whatever you find in the kitchen. Ms. Pip and Ned always stock the pantry before someone moves in." He turned and started up the stairs.

"Logan," I called, stopping him in his tracks. "Thank you for taking me in and for coming to dinner and—just thanks."

"Anytime."

He left, and I slumped on the floor next to the hope chest, my back against the chair. I pulled my cell phone out of my pocket and hit Dad's picture. It didn't ring on my end before he answered.

"I wasn't sure you'd call tonight," he said by way of a salutation.

I traced the faint letters on the box with my finger. "It's been a very long day."

"How'd it go?" he asked.

That's all it took. I told him about the drive, about Logan and then meeting Pip, Ned, and Fiona. I told him about Ned finding me all those years ago and coming to my graduation. I told him there was a video and Fiona had watched it on my birthday every year. About her quoting my speech. And dinner.

"Piper had dinner with me, Dad. Even though food makes her nauseous. Fiona told me Piper said she'd fed hundreds of kids in my name, so she was determined to feed me. That's what she did, Dad. She gave me to you and Mom, and ever since she's worked in my name. Amanda's Pantry. Fiona wasn't exaggerating. She did it for me. And all the books, they're dedicated to me. I feel . . ."

When I didn't say anything, Dad filled in, "Overwhelmed?"

"Yes. And humble. And maybe selfish."

"Selfish? How so?" he asked.

"I could have come sooner. Piper waited for me. And I could have come. I planned to find her, but life got in the way. I never felt like I was missing anything. I had you and mom. I was complete. But she was missing me."

"Siobhan, you're there now. You're being tested to see if you can help her. That's not selfish, sweetie. And I've always believed that things happen in their own time. You can't rush them. You simply have to take where you are and be content."

"Thus speaks the philosophy professor," I teased. Then seriously, I added, "I love you, Dad. No matter what, I need you. You do know that?"

"Honey, I do. I am not threatened by Piper. And if your mom were here, she wouldn't be, either. We had a discussion like this before, you know."

"I know. You said you and Mom would support me looking for Piper."

"No, not then. After we lost your mom and I introduced you to Margo. I was so afraid that you'd think I was replacing your mom. I could never do that. And loving Margo doesn't mean I loved your mom any less. You and Piper? It's sort of the same thing, and I understand that. When I told you about Margo, I said—"

"You said, that your heart was big enough to love someone else without displacing anyone," I quoted. I remembered that conversation and how nervous he had been.

"Hearts are elastic," he said. "I'm not sure the great philosophers would put it like that, but I think it's apt."

I needed this moment of talking to my dad. I still didn't know how I was feeling, but the swirling emotions had at least slowed down. "Thanks, Dad."

"It sounds as if you like these people, and that's good. It's a good place to start. And if you come to love them, I won't feel as if it means you love me any less. If your mom were here, she'd say the same thing."

"Thanks, Daddy." I hadn't called him that since I was younger than Fiona. It just slipped out. Maybe right now I wanted to be that little girl again.

When I was Fiona's age, life was simple. My parents adored me. I adored them. And because of them I knew I could be anything I wanted to be, and they'd be there for me. Like tonight, when I called Dad. He'd picked up before the phone rang on my end. He'd probably been sitting with it in his hand.

"Really, thanks, Dad. I love you. Good night."

"I love you, too. You call me tomorrow. And as soon as you hear from the doctors."

"I will," I promised.

I clicked the button and sat the phone down on the edge of the chest. It was easy to imagine people doing the same thing over the hundred-plus years it had been around.

I traced the letters again. T. P. E. I wondered who she was, this woman who'd originally owned the chest. And one day she'd passed it to her daughter. Then that daughter to her daughter and down the line. A line of women. Here I was on the other end of that line, and I knew nothing about them. Where they were from, what they're names were.

I was a math and science geek. Though I worked with technology, I remembered enough of my biology classes to think of mitochondrial DNA. It was the DNA that comes from someone's mother. It was microscopic bits that flowed down the river of time from one mother to the next. A long line of women, tied through time.

There was a very good chance that T. P. E's mitochondrial DNA flowed through Piper and through her to me. We were linked through blood. And if the poor odds landed in our favor, that blood might be able to help Piper. My bone marrow to be more specific.

60

I thought of that long line of women who'd come before me and hoped beyond hope that because of them I could save Piper.

I didn't open the chest. I also didn't sleep well.

The room I was using was comfortable enough. It was small, like so many bedrooms in older homes. I didn't mind that. I never thought a bedroom needed to have much more than a bed and a dresser or two in it. This one was adequate in that respect and had a small closet. It was painted a soothing light gray, and the bedding was a darker, steelier color.

No, it wasn't the room or the bed that caused my sleepless night. It wasn't even the chest that sat untouched in the living room. I was curious about Piper, but what I'd already learned was more than I could handle.

Every book she'd written she'd dedicated to me.

She'd started a food pantry in my name.

She'd never forgotten me.

She'd waited for me.

All night long those facts swirled around in my mind. I dreamed about her handing out food to babies. And in the dream, I saw her crying. A young girl, not much older than Fiona, crying.

I gave up pretending to sleep at 5:00. To be honest, I got up about that time most days. I'd always been an early bird. When friends bragged about sleeping away a weekend morning , I couldn't imagine it. I considered 6:00 a.m. sleeping in.

I'd slept in yoga pants and a tank top. I slipped my OSU sweatshirt on and felt I was modest enough for a roommate.

I wasn't sure if Logan was a light sleeper so I tiptoed past his door just in case, and then down the stairs, and into the kitchen. I turned on the small light in the hood over the stove and took him at his word and made myself at home. I hunted for the coffee. If I was going to stay for a while, I'd need to go to the grocery store, sooner rather than later.

Logan was right. The pantry was well stocked. I found the coffee and looked out the window as the coffeemaker chugged along.

Ned's backyard wasn't as jungle-esque as Piper's, but even in the morning murkiness I could see Piper's garden encroaching on his. I looked at the chestnut tree—Logan's tree. It looked sturdy in the corner.

When the coffee was done, I found a mug and padded out into the backyard. The ground was cold and dewy as I walked along the woodchip path, through the hole in the fence, and into Piper's backyard. I went to the bench we'd sat on yesterday and pulled my now freezing wet feet up onto the seat.

For a moment I sat in the silent morning but gradually realized it wasn't silent at all. I closed my eyes and listened to the sounds of it waking up. There was a bird feeder up closer to the house, and I could hear the birds calling out. A series of chirps, clicks, and whistles. I realized that the yard was a cacophony of sound.

Suddenly the sounds altered. The birds' calls grew shriller and then stopped abruptly. Seconds later, there was the sound of someone running on the path.

"I thought I saw you," Fiona said. "You're an early bird, like me. That makes sense 'cause we're sisters."

She was fully dressed, but she obviously hadn't brushed her hair. It stuck out this way and that from the remnants of yesterday's ponytail.

"If you sit here real quiet, you can hear my sparrows. They come to the feeder first thing every morning to check it out. If you're sitting closer to the house, you can see a couple come up and make sure there's feed, and then they call out to all the rest of them, and soon the feeder's swarming with them."

"You like birds?" I asked.

She nodded, sending more wisps of hair bolting from the ponytail holder. "Yeah. I like 'em all. When we used to go to the beach, I'd take bread for the seagulls. Logan says they're flying rats, but I like 'em. Did you ever read *Jonathan Livingston Seagull?* I think that's why," she said, not leaving me time to answer. "They've got snowy owls out on the peninsula now and bald eagles. And blue herons. Oh, and there's a whole part of the beach they close down every spring 'cause they hope some birds nest there. Plovers I think. I'd like to go to the peninsula and spot them, but Mom's not really up to that, so we just watch them back here. I got her garden certified as a wildlife habitat last year for her birthday. There's a little plaque near the house."

From where we sat at the back of the garden, the house was only just visible through the bushes and trees. In the summer, when all the leaves were full and green, I didn't think you'd be able to see it at all. "I'm sure Piper loved the present."

"I think so."

"I don't know much about bird songs, but I've always liked learning what groups of birds are called. They're all something different," I said. "A murder of crows, a raft of ducks, an unkindess of ravens." I thought about *Jonathan Livingston Seagull* and added, "a squabble of gulls."

"I didn't know those." Fiona paused and then went back to what was really on her mind. "She's really sick, you know."

"Yes."

"If you can't save her, then she might die," Fiona said, voicing my secret fear.

I didn't want the responsibility of saving Piper. It seemed like too much. But I couldn't say that to Fiona, so I warned her, "They said me being a match is a long shot."

"I know." She sighed. "I got tested, you know."

I shook my head. "I didn't."

"Mom said no, I was too young. So last spring, I got on a bus and went to her doctor's office. I told them I wanted to be tested.

63

Of course, they said no. I was a minor and they couldn't do any tests on me without my parents' permission. When they said that, I started crying. I mean, really crying. You know the kind of crying that when you start it you can't stop? That kind. It's so frustrating to be a kid and to have everyone think you can't understand and you can't help. I just couldn't stop. They were going to call Mom, but I made 'em call Dad. And when he showed up, I said if he didn't let me get tested, I was going to run away 'cause I couldn't live with knowing I might have saved her if they'd have just listened to me."

I looked at this young girl—my sister—with her sleep-tousled hair. She didn't sound nine. She sounded like an adult. I realized that for more than half of her life she'd lived with Piper's illness. She'd lived with the fears of losing her mother daily. It would be like living with a guillotine poised over your neck.

"I wasn't a match anyway," she said softly.

I set my coffee down on the bench next to me and reached over to her.

"They said kids aren't generally a match for their parents," Fiona said. "I think Grandma feels guilty. Like if maybe she'd had more kids, Mom would have a better chance."

I wondered about this grandmother I didn't know. Mom and Dad had both lost their parents before I came along, so I'd never had a grandparent.

"You tried. You did your best," I said, knowing how lame the words were even as I said them. "And I'm here to do mine. And if I'm not a match, either, maybe they'll find a donor out there."

She shrugged, and I could see in her expression that she didn't believe they'd find a donor. Rather than say so, Fiona said, "Mom will be up soon. Wanna come in and help me make her breakfast?"

"Do you think she'll mind me just making myself at home?"

"She's waited for you every day of your life. She gave me an Irish name because of yours. Siobhan and Fiona. We sound like sisters, don't we? Siobhan and Fiona." She said our names together as if she'd practiced them before.

I realized that she'd known about me her whole life. I felt bad about missing out on hers. A big sister should be there for a little one. And yet, Fiona was the one offering me comfort and support.

As if on cue, she added, "Mom loves you. She won't mind. She'll love it."

I nodded. I picked up my coffee cup and we walked toward the house. Fiona stopped. "Did you hear that?" she whispered.

"What?"

"There was a different bird call. Not a robin or sparrow. I'll tell Mom. We'll watch for it. She wrote *Fiona and the Magic Feather* for me, 'cause I loved birds so much."

With a different cadence to her voice, she said,

Fiona heard a call that she'd never heard before and ran to the feeder. She saw a feather resting on the ground. It was a very large feather. Blue and green and brown and black. The colors seemed to glow. She understood it was a very special gift . . . she was little enough to know magic when she saw it. Grownups were often too busy with the real world to notice that magic was real and that it was all around them.

I realized she was quoting the book.

"I believe in magic," she said. "I always believed you'd come home, and here you are. Magic." She opened the back door into the house.

I followed her in. "That must be so exciting to see your name in a book."

"It is." Fiona gave me a look that again was far too old for a nine-year-old. "But you know she wrote everything for you."

"I know. For Amanda," I said as we entered the kitchen. The sink and counter were filled with the remnants of last night's dinner dishes. I thought about Piper, making me a dinner despite the fact that food made her nauseous. It might be presumptuous to make myself at home, but I could at least get this cleaned up for her.

"Yeah, and—oh, you only read the older books. Hold on." She tore out of the kitchen and was back a few seconds later. "Here." She handed me a book called *The Naming of Things*. "This is one she wrote before I was born."

"To Siobhan . . . and Ned. You are my heart."

My hand trembled as I read the words. Piper had changed her dedications. She'd used my real name.

"And this one is after I was born." Fiona handed me another one. "For Ned, Siobhan, and my little Fiona."

"You have always been part of our family," Fiona told me. "Even before you knew us."

Fiona walked over to the pantry as if what she'd shown me was no big deal. I stood another moment, my finger tracing the letters of the dedication.

I felt another stab of guilt that I'd waited so long to come find Piper. And Ned and Fiona, too.

"I like to feed her healthy stuff," Fiona said.

I set the book aside as my sister and I—I realized I liked thinking that, *my sister and I*—made steel-cut oatmeal and finished cleaning the kitchen while it cooked.

When the last dish was put away, I said, "Why don't you go get a brush. I'll show you a braid my friend Jaylin used to do on my hair."

"Cool. Then we can make some fruit salad." Fiona dashed from the room almost silently. That she could move so quietly

66

didn't surprise me, I realized. She'd had a lot of practice as she tried not to disturb Piper.

Piper came down half an hour later and smiled when she saw me and Fiona sitting at the table, Fiona's new braid in place.

She ran her finger across Fiona's woven hair and said, "Beautiful."

"Siobhan did it. Her friend Jaylin used to do her hair like this. She's got lots of hair like we do. She says it's called a fishtail, but her and Jaylin always called it a Canadian braid 'cause Jaylin learned to do it from some Canadian girls at school. And when you got this much hair, a braid is always good."

"It is," Piper agreed and then added, "You cleaned the kitchen."

"Yep," Fiona said, willingly carrying the conversation. "Me and my sister are a good team."

Fiona bound from her chair and pulled out the one next to hers. "Sit down. Me and Siobhan made breakfast for you. She gets up early like me, and we were in the garden. I heard some new bird, so maybe later we can go out and see if we can spot it. Did you know a group of seagulls is a squabble?"

Piper sat down at the table. "No, I didn't."

I felt awkward and intrusive, though I already knew that Piper would deny both. "I hope you don't mind. Fiona thought—"

"This is your home, Siobhan," Piper said simply, though there was nothing simple about meeting her, meeting all of them.

Piper managed a few bites of her oatmeal. I think she only managed that much for Fiona's sake. I could see that it was taxing. She didn't look like someone who'd just gotten out of bed. She looked exhausted.

"Can I get you something?" I asked softly as Fiona ran to get her a bowl of fruit salad.

"Maybe you should go get Ned. I think there's a chance I need to get to the doctor's. I think I'm running a bit of a fever."

"Hey, Fiona, would you go ask your dad to come down?" I called.

Fiona looked at me, then Piper, and then bolted from the room without saying a word.

"I'm so sorry," Piper said. "You're finally here. All I want to do is sit somewhere quiet and pepper you with questions. I want to know about your childhood, what you do now. I want to know about your best friend. Instead—"

"We'll have time, Piper," I promised her and maybe myself. "I have questions, too."

"I tried to answer most of them in the journal. I wanted to be sure that whenever you came to find me there was something for you. I'm glad I wrote it. If something should happen to me—"

"Don't talk like that." I'd just met Piper, but already the thought of a world without her in it hurt.

She patted my hand, trying to give me comfort. "Honey, everyone dies someday. I want you to know that I never forgot you. I might have given you to your parents, but I built a life around you. You were always loved."

I wanted to tell her that I loved her, too. But I didn't know her well enough for that. I could tell her I wanted to love her and yet was afraid to love her.

"I—" I didn't have time to say anything. Ned and Fiona rushed into the room. He took one look at Piper and simply picked up the phone and called the doctor.

"We're going to meet him at the hospital," he said when he'd hung up.

"I don't want—"

I took Piper's hand and squeezed it. "We'll have time. Go see the doctor."

Then an idea occurred to me. "Why don't I take Fiona? I mean, I understand if you'd prefer she go with someone else. You hardly know me."

"She's your sister," Piper said. In her expression I could see how formidable she must have been before she got sick. "Of course you can take her for the day."

I wanted to argue against this basic trust she put in me. I knew I was trustworthy, but how could she?

"I checked you out, remember?" Ned said, answering my unasked question.

I nodded. "She mentioned wanting to see some birds on the peninsula. I thought we'd make a day of it."

"Thank you. I wish I could be there," Piper said. "I want—"

"We'll have days," I promised her again. "Many days. A lifetime of days," I said, willing it to be true.

She nodded, accepting my words as truth, even though neither of us could know if they were.

"I love you," she said, as Ned led her from the kitchen.

Chapter Four

Susan walked down the beach, leaving the lifeguards and swimmers behind her. Slowly the sand gave way to rocky sand and finally to just rocks. And the sounds of radios and children screaming gave way to the sounds of the waves and an occasional seagull.

She turned the bend, sat on a giant boulder, and stared out at the lake, her feet resting on a huge piece of driftwood.

THE GREAT LAKE. She thought the words in all caps because from where she sat, Lake Erie felt as big as an ocean. And because it seemed so big, she felt dwarfed by it. Small. And suddenly so did all her problems.

They felt smaller and more manageable.

All she had to do was sit here, alone at the water's edge, and watch the waves and the seagulls. She didn't have to worry about—

"Hi, Susan."

She turned, and he smiled at her as he sat down next to her. So much for not worrying.

—Susan's Summer, by Pip

We saw Ned and Piper out to the car, and then Fiona and I cleaned up the breakfast dishes. Her optimism seemed to deflate as her mother left.

70

"It's happened before. Lots of times," she said. "She gets sick so easy. But she always gets better."

I could almost hear her think *until one day when she won't.* I could almost hear it because I felt the same way.

I went next door and Logan was up. "I wondered where you went to," he said with a smile that slipped as he studied me. "What happened?"

"Piper's sick. Ned's taking her to the hospital to meet the doctor, so I'm taking Fiona to the peninsula for the day. Want to come?"

I glossed over Piper being sick because I didn't want Logan to worry. He hadn't seen her, but I had. And I was worried enough for the both of us.

He gave me a look. An intense sort of look.

It was as if he could see what I was thinking. It was as if he could see the whirling emotions that I couldn't seem to slow or even begin to sort out. But he looked as if he could. So he didn't press and ask me more about Piper. He simply said, "My shift doesn't start until seven tonight, so sure, if you don't mind me intruding."

"You wouldn't be. Fiona seems happy to get to know me, but still, I'm a stranger. I think she'll be more comfortable having someone familiar along."

Logan snorted. "Fiona has never met a stranger, and even if she had, you wouldn't be one. You've been part of her life for as long as she can remember. Not just the birthday parties. I babysat for her sometimes, and she says her prayers every night. You're always in them. It sounds like a simple thing but it's not. Every night, she thought about you and hoped you were happy. That's pretty powerful. So, no, you're not a stranger to Fiona. But, yes, I'd love to tag along. Let me go get changed." He left and went back up the stairs.

I started to go as well, but the chest that was still under the window caught my eye. I walked over and ran my hand over the top, tracing the faded lettering T. P. E.

71

I thought about opening it but didn't. I wasn't sure why, but I couldn't bring myself to. I was curious about what Piper had put in it. I'd read the excerpt of the journal that Ned had given me. What other stories had she told me in it?

I turned away from the chest and hurried upstairs to get ready. I didn't bother to put a bathing suit on. It was too late in the season for me to want to swim. But I grabbed a towel and wore some capris I could easily cuff.

Logan came down in shorts, an Mercyhurst University T-shirt, and a small sports bag thrown over his shoulder.

"Want me to drive?" he asked. "I know the way."

"Thanks. If you do, I won't need my GPS then." Fiona was out front in shorts and a T-shirt that read *Fi Fly Flo* and had a picture of a unicorn on it. I wondered if she'd chosen the shirt to feel closer to Piper. I didn't ask, but I did tug at her braid. "Logan said he'd drive since he knows the way."

"Great!"

Fiona was a mini-encyclopedia of knowledge. She spent the drive telling us that Presque Isle peninsula was once the home of the Eriez Nation. It was defeated by the Iroquois , but the name stuck to the lake and the city. The Eriez had a legend of the Sheltering Arm of the Great Spirit, who they believed sent them to the peninsula for the abundant wildlife, the clean water, and the cool summer breezes.

She said that there was a chance we'd see some migratory birds today. The peninsula was a frequent stop for many of them. "Maybe we'll see some eagles or osprey," she said in a tone that most kids would use about Christmas.

"She likes birds," Logan said as he drove past a local amusement park. I could see a huge Ferris wheel, and then we passed under a section of rollercoaster track.

"I remember coming to Waldameer when I was a girl," I said. "But I don't remember the rollercoaster coming out over the road."

"It used to, but then they tore it down years ago," Logan said. "The park just put it back a few years ago. I haven't ridden in it yet. Too bad the park's closed for the season or we'd stop."

"We'll go in the spring," Fiona said. "Logan'll be here because of school, and you're gonna come visit a lot, right?"

"Yes," I assured her. "It's not too bad a drive. I'll come visit so much you'll get sick of me."

She shook her head. "Nope. I waited my whole life for you. I won't get sick of you."

Her words reminded me of what Logan had said. "You're my sister, Fiona. Even when I go home, you can always call me, and we can Skype."

"Really?" she asked.

"Really," I assured her.

That seemed to satisfy her. She went back to her running history of the park. She had the same sense of wonder and excitement of a tour guide.

She made us drive out to the end of the peninsula and loop around to Beach 11. "It's shallow like forever here," she explained.

She ran out on to the beach, threw her bag down, stripped off her shoes, and raced down to the water. She was up to her knees before Logan and I had made it to her bag.

"Come on in," she called.

"I'll come stick a toe in," I called back. "But I don't think I'm doing much more than that."

"Me, too," Logan echoed.

We stood in ankle-deep water and watched Fiona as she cavorted in the shallows.

"She seems to be doing okay," I marveled. "I can't help worrying about Piper."

"Fi's grown up with Ms. Pip's illness. She wasn't even in school when it all started. This is normal for her."

"It's not fair," I whispered.

"I've spent the last few years working at clinics all over the world. I've seen so much . . . ," he paused and his voice was shaky as he continued. "There's so much need, Siobhan. I could work the rest of my life and never make a dent in the need that's out there. I said as much to Ms. Pip one day. I felt like I was tossing tiny pebbles into the ocean during a storm. The water's already churning so much the pebble doesn't make even the tiniest of a ripple. You know what she said?"

"What?"

"No one person can ever fix all the world's hurts. All we can do is our best to change our corner of it. She said that's what she does with Amanda's Pantry and even with her books." His voice changed, and he quoted her.

I mean, I realize my little stories won't end world hunger, but maybe for a few minutes, someone who's hurting is comforted. Maybe someone who's sad smiles or even laughs. And even if a sad part in my book makes a reader cry, maybe that's cathartic. Maybe they don't feel quite as alone. And maybe that's enough.

"I never thought about things like that," I said. I remembered reading Piper's books when I was growing up. I felt connected to her characters, like they knew me; like they understood what I was going through.

Logan laughed. "Yeah, making you think is something she's good at. She asked me something about what if everyone tossed their own pebble into the sea in some way? Then she said she thought maybe life would be a whole lot sweeter. So, that's what I do. Wherever I'm at, I just try to toss my pebble into the ocean. Life will never be fair, but we can all try to make our corner of it a bit better. You're doing that today for Fiona."

"I'm not doing anything," I said. Fiona reached into the water and held up something I couldn't make out.

"Beach glass," Logan filled in for me. "And you are doing something. You're here with her. Spending a day with her. She's waited to meet you for so long, you being here is making things easier."

"*Shove*, come in," Fiona said.

"Ban," I corrected. "If you're going to shorten my name, Ban's much better than Shove."

She laughed as I reached down and cuffed my pants and waded farther into the water.

"Are you coming?" I called to Logan.

"Go ahead and bond with your sister. I'm going to catch a catnap."

"Ban," Fiona called, trying my nickname on for size. "Why that?"

"Think about how my name is spelled. A teacher pronounced it Ceo-ban. The *ban* part stuck."

"I like it," she said. "Ban. Okay. Fi and Ban. Mom can write a book for us when she's better. She'll . . ."

She went on, deciding that Ban, being Irish, was Fi's best friend. And she wove book-worthy adventures for them as we walked down the beach. "Watch for beach glass," she instructed.

Logan, good to his word, had spread out a towel and lain down on it. He seemed to be dead to the world. "He barely woke up and he's napping," I said to Fiona.

"When he works nights, he takes a morning then an afternoon nap. He works per diem at the hospital whenever he's in town."

"Is he here often?" I asked, glancing back at his inert form on the empty beach. It was late in the season for swimmers. I liked having this little corner of the lake to ourselves.

She shrugged. "Yeah, I guess he's home a few times a year. Sometimes he stays with his mom, sometimes next door. He's been all over the world, you know. He sends me postcards in the real old fashioned mail. But he e-mails and Skypes, too. He's been everywhere. I've got a map on the computer that we mark off every time he goes somewhere new. He was in South America once and worked at a place that helps kids with cleft palates. Have you ever seen them? It's easier to fix 'em when they're babies, but sometimes they're as old as me and still got them. And then—"

The more Fiona told me, the more I realized that Logan hadn't just thrown a pebble in the ocean of human suffering. He'd already thrown a big handful of rocks.

Fiona reached into the water and came up with something. She opened her hand and showed me a piece of green beach glass and then shoved it in her pocket. "When I get older, I'm going to be a photojournalist and travel to all those places and take pictures. I always make Logan send me some. Seeing the people he helps makes it more real, you know?"

I nodded. "Yes, I think I understand."

Before Ned had knocked on my door, I'd known in an academic sense that I had a biological mother somewhere. I knew that she'd given me to my parents to raise and in so doing had given me a wonderful gift.

But now that I'd met her, as well as Ned and Fiona, Piper wasn't just *something* I knew. She was real. Her pain was real. And I'd do whatever I could to help her.

"You can come over, and I'll show you the pictures if you like," Fiona was saying.

"I'd like that."

Fiona gave me a look and said, "You know, you should be his girlfriend. If you were, then he'd be my brother, and he's always been like one so that would be cool."

I choked on absolutely nothing but air. "Well, Logan and I just met, so I don't think we're quite ready to be more than friends." I looked back at him and said, "But sometimes a friend is better than a boyfriend."

"Why?" she asked.

"Because boyfriends come and go, but real friends are like family, they stick around."

She looked like she was thinking, and then she nodded. "Yeah, that's good then. Me and Logan are friends, and now you can be, too. But I'm your sister."

"Yes," I assured her. "You are my sister."

We spent the rest of the morning on the beach. Fiona found a small handful of beach glass. We all admired them. She pointed to the browns and greens. "Those are my favorites. They remind me of Mom's garden."

After Fiona got dressed again, we went for a hike on one of her favorite paths. She listed off the birds she wanted to find, but we didn't see anything spectacular according to her.

In my opinion, all the birds we did see were all pretty amazing.

We went back to the house, got lunch, and Fiona ran to a neighbor's house.

Ned texted as Logan and I did the dishes, *Pip's being admitted. Everything okay there?*

It's fine here. Tell Piper she's in our thoughts.

"It'll be okay, Siobhan. This isn't the first time," Logan said very sensibly.

I didn't feel sensible. It didn't seem fair that I'd finally met Piper only to have her taken out of reach. "I know it's a Sunday so I won't hear anything today, but I want to know if I'm a match. If I am—"

"Even if you are, there's a lot to do," Logan said. "You'll have a battery of tests to go through to be sure you're healthy enough to donate. Ms. Pip will have to recover from whatever this setback is, and then she'll have to go through some pretty intense chemo before she could have the transplant."

"But I—"

He interrupted me by taking my hand and pulling me toward the front door. "Come sit with me."

Archie barked at the door. "He can come out," Logan said. "He knows the drill."

Archie curled into a ball in the corner of the porch, content to be outside with us.

It was late afternoon, and there was a touch of a chill in the air, a reminder that autumn was just around the corner.

"I love this house," Logan said, sparing me from coming up with anything conversational. "You know, I asked Ms. Pip why she didn't move. I mean, this is a nice enough neighborhood, but I suspect she could afford to live in one of the more expensive neighborhoods in town." He laughed. "I know, it's presumptuous to speculate on someone else's income, but it was a number of years ago, so I'll offer up youth as an excuse."

"What did she say?" I asked.

"She said, *This is home. Why would I want to live anywhere else?*" He looked at me, and I realized that his dark eyes were actually blue. A very deep grayish blue. Rather like the color of the lake. They stood out against his dark complexion and hair.

"You're in Ms. Pip's chair right now," he said. "I grew up seeing her sit there. It's where she liked to work."

"Don't use past tense," I said.

He nodded. "She'll work here again. But it's been about a year since she wrote something. I know that I'm not the only one who misses seeing her sit here every day."

The chair felt comfortable, and the porch railing was close enough that I could easily extend my feet and prop my legs against it. My laptop would sit nicely on my thighs if I did. "I can imagine that this would be a good place to work."

"Ms. Pip's a fixture. A generation of kids have watched her working in the nice weather and right behind that window," he pointed to the window just behind the chairs, "in the colder weather. But you could count on her. She'd wave every day. And if you told her you were worried about a test, or about anything, she'd ask you about it. She genuinely cared. Not just the food pantry stuff. She volunteered as the kindergarten story lady, you know."

"Fiona said something about her at school."

"She went into the classes once a week or so and read the kids a couple of books. Sometimes they were her books. She says the kindergarten kids were a great testing ground. But she also had stacks of favorites. The one I remember best was *Where the Wild Thing Are*. She came in for a whole afternoon. We read the book, and afterward we made our own wild-thing masks. She had this huge box of stuff. Glitter. Fabric. Tinsel. We had markers, glue, and we went a bit nuts. But so did she. When we finished, we all wore our masks and she read the story again. This time, she had her *wild-rumpus* music, and we all howled and gnashed our teeth and showed our claws."

I could almost picture Piper—the Piper from the Internet photo—wearing a mask, her red hair flaming above it as she howled and gnashed with the kids. "It sounds like she had as much fun as the kids."

"She got so excited about everything. She made everything special," Logan said.

"Makes," I corrected.

He nodded. "Makes. What was your childhood like?" he asked changing directions.

I realized he hadn't really told me about his childhood, just the Piper part, but I didn't press. "I had a wonderful childhood. I was an only child of two educators, so the house was full of books. *Where the Wild Things Are* is probably still in the attic somewhere. And *Little Women* and the Trixie Belden books, and *Anne of Green Gables*. I fell in love with Prince Edward Island. When I was about

79

Fiona's age, my parents took me there for a summer vacation."
I realized I'd talked about Anne and PEI last night. "Sorry, I'm
being redundant."

"I don't mind hearing about them again. I never read them,"
he said.

"I guess they weren't high on a boy's reading list," I said with
a laugh.

"Your parents sound nice."

"They were. They doted on me, but I don't think they spoiled
me . . . at least not too much." My happiness had come at Piper's
expense.

Again, as if he could read my thoughts, Logan said, "That's
what Ms. Pip always wanted for you. After Fiona invited me to
your party, we talked about you. Me and Ms. Pip. She said she
gave you away because you deserved so much more than she
could have given you then. She wanted you to have the kind of
childhood she had. Wait until you meet your grandparents."

I wasn't ready to meet anyone else. But I didn't say so. Logan
let me be. We sat in silence on the porch, and I tried to imagine
Piper sitting in this chair, watching a generation of children across
the street at the school.

At some point, I realized he was holding my hand. It was as if
he knew I needed to feel connected to someone.

I'd only known Logan Greer for a bit more than a day, but he
already felt like someone I could count on.

Like a friend.

I didn't pull away.

Chapter Five

Simone had two coats. One was soft and light blue. It fell to her knees. She liked the way it swished against her legs as she walked. The other coat was a fat down coat that made her look like a bright yellow marshmallow but kept her warm no matter how long she was outside.

She was wearing her marshmallow coat on Saturday—along with her bright yellow-and-orange hat and gloves—when she went to the park to sled. She felt bright and warm and excited to spend a day out in the snow. Then she noticed Lena D. from school. She was wearing a hooded sweatshirt and a black knit hat. And no gloves.

—*The Marshmallow Coat*, by Pip

Over the next few days, we all fell into a routine. Ned had worked for a law firm for years, but when Piper got sick, he'd cut back at work. The firm had hired a new full-time investigator, so Ned worked per diem when Piper's health allowed. He also picked up work from other people when he could.

I wondered how they managed financially. I didn't know much about writing, but I assumed that Piper had enough coming in from her books to support the family. I thought about what Logan had said when he asked about why they lived here.

81

They lived simply enough. Maybe her career had prepared them both for uncertain incomes.

I lived the same way. When APPlicable sold its first few apps, I'd taken my share of the money and squirreled it away. I continued living as if I were college poor until one day I realized that I had a nice nest egg. I invested that in a house that cost half what the bank prequalified my loan for. I lived frugally, building up a cushion that would tide me over if the business took a downturn.

Although Ned wasn't working, he spent most days at the hospital with Piper. I went every day as well to give Ned a break. Piper was too exhausted to visit, but I think she liked seeing me.

I made sure I was at the house when Fiona got home from school. If Logan wasn't working or at school, the three of us had dinner together. If he was gone, it was just Fiona and me. Either way, I stayed with her until Ned got home.

Fiona's grandparents—my grandparents—had offered to keep her, but Fiona insisted she wanted to stay with me. I'd met them. They seemed nice enough. I met Piper's friend, Cooper, too. But the two people I was really getting to know were Fiona and Logan.

I'd come to meet my mother, but I felt as if I'd developed a closer bond with the sister I hadn't known I had and my inadvertent roommate.

Ned got home Friday night at almost eight. I jumped off the couch as I heard him open the door. We met near the doorway. "Is Fi still up?"

I nodded. "Last I saw her she was heading up to take a bath. I hope you don't mind, but I bought her an orange spa kit."

"I don't know what that is," he said with a smile that didn't reach his eyes. No, in his eyes I saw utter exhaustion and maybe the first hints of fear.

"Bubbles for the bath and lotion. She likes the smell of mine, so I got her one. She misses Piper, and I thought a little treat was in order." If I knew him better, I might hug him. But I didn't know him well enough for that, so I tucked my hands in my pockets.

"Piper misses her," he said. "She misses everyone. She's so torn up that you're here and she's stuck in the hospital."

"How is she . . . ," I paused and added, "really?"

"She's getting sicker."

"I called my doctor again to get the results. He said soon. Hopefully in the next few days." I paused and asked, "What are we going to do if I'm not able to donate."

Ned seemed to freeze a moment, as if my question caught him unaware. He fiddled with a picture on a shelf. It was of Fiona as a toddler, wearing a plaid jumper and shiny black Mary Jane shoes.

He turned to me and answered, "We'll keep hoping they find a donor out there. People join the registry every day. I know that before Pip got sick, I never gave it a thought, but now I give thanks every day for all the selfless people who have signed up. It takes a special kind of person to be willing to do something like that for a stranger. People who are willing to give of themselves—literally—for someone else."

"There haven't been any matches yet, though," I said.

He forced a smile and squared his shoulder. "That doesn't mean there won't be one tomorrow."

Maybe sometimes, when you're scared to your core, finding the will to act brave is an act of bravery in itself.

I reached out and patted his forearm. "I'll see you in the morning."

"Siobhan, if you need to get home . . . ," he started but trailed off as I shook my head.

"I can work here as easily as there. And I think right now I need to be here." I paused and added, "I want to be here as long as you don't mind."

He hugged me. "Mind? No. Pip would be able to come up with a word that is the direct opposite of *mind*, but I can't. I'll just say that we're thankful that you are here. I just don't want you to think we're taking advantage of you. You've been such a help with Fi, but I know you have your own life."

"Ned, I didn't know I had a sister. And even if I had, I don't think I could have been prepared for Fiona." She was a force of nature. "She's amazing. She had birthday parties for me. She showed me the pictures of them."

He nodded. "She made me take a picture of your cake every year, and she started her scrapbook. We look at them every year."

"I couldn't leave her like this. She's aching for Piper, and I can't change that, but I can be here for her and try to make it easier."

"You have made it easier. Thank you. I'm not sure any of us have remembered to say it enough, but thank you."

I started for the door, but he said, "Siobhan, I've read those articles about nature versus nurture over the years. I never paid much attention to the debate. But since I've met you, I've decided that I believe in both. Your parents raised you to be a loving, caring woman. But I think there's a chance that you inherited the size of your heart from Piper. She says that everything she's done was for you, and I know you were the impetus, but I suspect that even without being nudged in that direction, she would have done those things. It's in her nature. And I see so much of that nature in you. That doesn't mean I don't appreciate everything you've done. Thank you."

I didn't know what to say to that, so I simply nodded and hurried out the door. Rather than go back to the house next door, I walked along the side of the house and let myself in the garden gate.

I walked to the bench by the milkweed. There were small solar lights along the now well-trodden path. They provided enough light to outline the path, though I suspected that even a month ago, when the trees were thick with leaves, the lights were less useful.

I wondered if there was any way to find lights that had a collection panel that could be moved to a sunnier location and still power the shady garden lights next summer.

I'd have to look into it. I suspected Piper would love to have a more sustainable lighting source next year.

A tiny voice in my head added, *if she's still here.*

I sat on the bench and looked back at Piper, Ned, and Fiona's house. There was a light on in the kitchen, and one shining from the upstairs hall. I could imagine Ned and Fiona sitting together and talking about Piper. Fiona was worried. He'd reassure her.

I heard someone on the path coming from my backyard through the hole in the fence.

"I saw Ned's car come in, and when you didn't come home, I suspected I'd find you here."

Logan sat down next to me on the small bench. His thigh was pressed against my thigh; his arm, pressed against mine. "How is she?" he asked.

Neither of us needed to clarify who *she* was. "Holding her own."

"Would you like me to move the chest she gave you up to your room?"

I shook my head. Even in the gloom of the night garden, he saw my gesture. Quietly, he asked, "Have you opened it yet?"

I sighed. "No."

"Why not?"

I wasn't sure how to answer the question because to be honest, I didn't know. I'd looked at the hope chest so many times. I'd traced T. P. E. again and again.

I finally said, "Piper wrote me a journal that's in there, along with presents she'd bought me over the years. She wrote the journal so that I'd know her. But that's not how I want to find out about her. I want her to tell me. I want to hang out with her and get to know her in person like I'm getting to know Fiona and Ned and you. If I read the journal, it's like I'm admitting she'll never be around for me to get to know in person."

Logan didn't make light of my feelings. He simply reached over and pulled me into his arms. "I have an idea."

I was tired. Too tired to come up with any new ideas of my own. Jaylin knew me well enough that she was sending me only minimal work. I knew that meant she was picking up the slack, but I was too tired to argue with that, too.

"What's your idea?"

"Come out with me tomorrow."

For one second I thought he was asking me on a date, but then he added, "I'm volunteering at Ms. Pip's food pantry. It's been a few years since Ms. Pip's been well enough to run things. Cooper has taken over the management, and a lot of Ms. Pip's kids have volunteered to help."

I nodded. "I'd like that."

I would like to see the food pantry that Piper had opened in my name.

"And, Siobhan, you should open the chest."

I tugged at the locket I still wore daily around my neck. "I will, just not yet."

We sat quietly for a long time.

There was something soothing about the garden. The leaves rustled. I'd never thought about it, but the sound of leaves changes. In the summer, there's a soft brushing noise when they rub together in the breeze. Like a cotton shirt that brushes against the closet door as you take it out. But now, as we approached mid-September, the leaves weren't as lush and soft as they had been. They were tired and changing colors. It was as if they sent all the vibrancy into that change, and afterward they were simply tired and dried out. The sound they made was louder, and I knew as the season progressed and they dried out more, they would become louder yet. Would I still be here to witness that change?

The harder question was, would Piper still be here?

The next day, I went over to Piper's early. Fiona was still asleep, so I made myself at home. It was easier now. I didn't feel like such an interloper.

I started to do some basic chores. I wasn't sure where things went. If I couldn't make an educated guess, then I piled them up on the table at the bottom of the stairs, hoping Fiona would take care of them.

She did. She took a pile of clean clothes upstairs, and then she came down with a huge box.

"Hey, we're cleaning up, not getting out," I teased.

She laughed. "This is going next door with you."

"What is it?" I asked.

"I asked Mom about getting you copies of her newer books. She said that there are older ones in the chest, but it was full, so she started a box in the attic. She told me where to find it and . . ." She thrust the heavy box into my arms. "Here."

I set it down and opened it. There was a copy of *The Marshmallow Coat*. The picture on the cover was of a girl with dark braids wearing a vibrant yellow coat that did look remarkably marshmallow-esque.

"Open it," Fiona said.

I did. On the dedication page it read, "For Ned, Siobhan, and Fiona." Underneath in her handwriting was a note.

Dear Siobhan,

I hope you've never been hungry or cold. I hope your life has been filled with laughter, warmth, and love. Know you'll always have a home here.

Piper

I closed the book, put it back in the box, and shut the lid.

"Thank you, Fiona," I managed shakily.

"Let's take them over to your house and get Logan. We need to get to the food pantry early."

Piper had saved and signed each of her books for me.

Emotions began to swirl, but I pushed them down. Maybe when Piper was better, I'd have time to pull out each emotion and analyze it, but for now I tucked them away. We went next door and found Logan sipping his coffee.

"Are you ready?" he asked, looking excited.

"Sure. Let me put these upstairs before we go." I'd put them in my room and go through them later.

My room.

I realized that this room at the end of the hall did indeed feel like my room. Just as I felt at home at Piper and Ned's.

One week.

I'd only been here a week, and yet so much had happened that it felt longer.

I went downstairs, and the three of us walked across the street, through the school parking lot, to the school room Amanda's Pantry used every other week.

I patted my pocket and realized I'd forgotten my phone. Most days I'd run back and get it—I hated feeling unconnected. But since coming here, I'd been overwhelmed by connections. Giving myself a break from the phone didn't seem like a bad idea.

I paused a moment and looked at the school. It looked like so many other schools. The windows of each classroom were decorated for the new school year. The top floor windows had construction paper letters that spelled out W E L C O M E F A L L.

I thought about all the years Piper had come here, not just for the food pantry, but also to read to the kindergarten class.

Logan reached out and squeezed my hand. "Are you okay?"

I smiled and nodded, though we both knew that was a lie. It wasn't that I didn't want to be honest; it was simply that I couldn't be.

Logan and Fiona were old pros at setting up for the day. I followed their lead, though I suspected I was more in the way than helpful.

The first person through the door that day was a young mom and a young boy. I'd never been around enough kids to guess his age, but he was definitely a few years younger than Fiona.

"Hi, I'm Jerome," said the gap-toothed boy clutching a manila envelope.

I grinned. "Hi, Jerome. I'm Siobhan."

"D'you know Ms. Pip?" he asked.

I nodded. "I do."

"Good." He thrust an envelope at me. "Would ya give her these?"

"I will," I promised.

"Good," he said again. "She's been sick, so me and the club wanted her to see our grades 'cause they'll make her feel better. Mr. Kyle said we're all rock stars, and I said, no, we're all math stars."

He walked over to Fiona, presumably to share his math-star status with her, and his mother smiled at me. "Ms. Pip found out that Jerome was having trouble with math, so she talked to one of the teachers, and he put together a math club. They meet once a week. There are fourteen kids in it now. They met all summer. Last week was their first test of the year, and . . ." She nodded at the stack of papers. "Every one of them got an A. They wanted to be sure Piper knew."

"I'll take them over to the hospital tonight," I promised.

"Any news on a donor?" she asked.

Every time my phone rang, my heart leaped, thinking this was it, a message from my doctor. Every time it wasn't.

I shook my head.

"We all got tested and joined the registry in her name."

Logan reached under the table and took my hand. I nodded. "I'm sure she's touched. And I know that she's going to feel so much better after she sees the math tests."

"You tell her we're all praying for her," Jerome's mother said.

That set the tone for the day. A lot of the clients knew Logan and stopped to talk to him. That was always a relief because they didn't ask me any uncomfortable questions.

Every time Fiona heard me introduce myself as a friend of the family, she looked disappointed.

The last visitor of the day was a beautiful teenaged girl. "Hey, Logan," she called as Fiona rushed up to her and threw herself at the girl.

"Lovey," Fiona cried.

The girl came up to the table, Fiona still hanging on her, and asked Logan, "How long are you back for?"

"The school year. I'm going to stay in town and finish the program."

As he said the words, I could see that staying in town for the school year was going to be hard on him. He had a look in his eye, as if he were thinking about some faraway, exotic place. I knew just the word to describe his look . . . *wanderlust.*

"Nice," the girl said.

"Lovey this is Siobhan. Siobhan, this is Lovey Ridley."

She laughed. "No one calls me Lovey except my mom and everyone here. I stopped by today to send Ms. Pip something."

"We've got a collection," he said, pointing at the box we'd started for all the notes, tests, and the other small gifts.

Lovey pulled a newspaper out of her bag. "I wrote an essay last spring for a competition. It won. The prize was a savings bond for college. Well, the school newspaper reprinted it on the front page. It's about Amanda's Pantry and Ms. Pip. I thought it might make her smile."

"I'm sure it will," Logan assured her.

Lovey placed the paper in the box with the rest of the collection. "Tell her to get better soon. We miss her."

"I will." I promised.

I felt like I was perpetually on the verge of tears seeing how many people Piper had touched.

When Ned came to take Fiona to the hospital to see Piper, we sent the box of letters and gifts with them.

Logan and I cleaned up and then locked the door. We walked back across the street.

"Do you have some time?" he asked.

"Sure. Why?"

He opened up his car door. "Get in."

I did, and he started driving.

"Where are we going?"

"Do you trust me?" he asked.

I'd only known the man a week, but I realized that I did indeed trust him. I nodded. He glanced from the road to me in time to see it.

"Good."

We drove in silence to wherever he was taking me. That might have been awkward with some people, but it was comfortable with Logan. Before I knew it, he parked his car near the bay. "Let's go."

We walked between the bay and a huge hotel. There was a wall that separated the walkway and the water. Birds perched on it and an occasional fisherman.

Across the bay I could see the arch of the peninsula. The beach we had visited was on the lake side. The side I could see now was lined with trees. Pops of color accentuated the dark green leaves.

There was one lone sailboat on the water. I wondered how much longer it would be able to go out before it got too cold. Tonight finally felt like autumn. It wasn't cold, but rather it was cool.

I reached up and realized my nose was cold.

Logan stopped suddenly and pointed at the wall. "Look."

There was enough light from the streetlights to make out that each brick that made up the wall had someone's name on it. Logan pointed to a specific one.

"It was a fundraiser," he explained.

Piper George, simply ERIEsistible.

"The kids at the pantry raised money to buy it for her. The Eriesistible was a play on an old tourism campaign here. I thought you might like to see it."

"Thank you." I ran my finger over the chiseled stone and felt another small connection to her.

We walked along the bay, and Logan took my hand but didn't say a word. As we walked, I realized that this was just what I needed. The sound of the water and the seagulls. The cold nose. Even holding hands, that nondemanding connection that reminded me that I wasn't alone.

As we finished our walk, I realized something else. Logan understood me better in a week than Carey had understood me in eight years.

"Thank you," I said as we pulled into the driveway. "I needed that."

As if to emphasize my last thought, he nodded. "I thought you might."

He took my hand again as we walked to the front door. "I'm going up to my room for a bit," I said.

He smiled and nodded.

I went up to my room and saw the box of Piper's books on the bed. I found my cell phone just where I'd left it. I had three messages. One was from my dad. One from Carey. And one from a number I didn't recognize. I played that last one first.

I'm not sure how long I stood there holding my phone, but the next thing I knew, Logan was standing in the doorway and looking at me with concern. "Siobhan, are you okay."

I nodded as I looked up at him. "I'm more than okay."

I paused a moment, trying to let the news sink in. "I'm a match."

Part Two: October

Chapter Six

Hearts expand as needs be. They never truly run out of room. And despite popular belief, they never break. They can bruise, but given time and attention they will heal.
—*A Four Letter Word: Love*, by Pip

When I was little, I was prone to night terrors. I never remembered what I'd dreamed about. To be honest, I don't really remember having them. What I do remember is waking up, feeling hot, sweaty, and so scared. And every time, I'd also find my mother curled up next to me on the bed. She'd be stroking my hair and murmuring *shh* or *it's all right*.

Eventually I outgrew those night terrors, but my dream life was an active one. I'd kept a dream journal for years simply because the act of writing my dreams down solidified them in my mind. I didn't really analyze them or believe they would lead me to some greater truth, but I did believe that sometimes I worked things out in a dream, things I'd never have thought about in the light of day.

Sometimes the dreams made no sense. And sometimes they made all kinds of sense. The night after my surgery, I dreamed.

I dreamed about a dirty-looking little girl with red hair. She was me, and yet she wasn't me at all. I saw her sitting at an empty table, and then I saw Piper sweep into the room. This was Piper from the Internet, all smiles and strength with long red hair. She pulled the grubby child onto her lap, sang a song to her, and rocked her.

Then my mom walked into the room and said, "Thank you." Piper looked up and said, "Take care of her."

She handed me/the little girl to my mom, who walked away. But though I'd been the girl who my mother carried away, I was still in the room with Piper who sat at the table and cried as if her heart would break.

I reached for her, but I couldn't touch her. I couldn't help her. She faded right before my eyes. She tied a scarf over her head, covering her hair, and then she turned pale, thinned, and then turned into a misty gray figure, losing solidity as I watched. She handed me Fiona and said, "It's your turn now. Take care of her."

And then I was sitting on top of the hope chest, rocking Fiona who was suddenly an infant with red hair. I cried and said, "I don't know how to do this."

And then I woke up.

"Ban, wake up," someone said.

I woke up and found myself wrapped in Logan's arms.

"Shh," he said as he stroked my hair in the same way my mother once had, but the feelings his touch evoked were not filled with childlike innocence at all.

"It's all right. You're not alone," he murmured.

"I feel as if I am," I admitted. "I feel as if I'm going to lose Piper when I've only just found her. I feel as if all the talks I've wanted to have with her will never happen. I feel as if all I'll be able to do is see her through a glass wall or with a mask over my face."

"You're not going to lose her," he said with more confidence than I felt. "Can I get you something? A drink?"

I shook my head. "My mother always did that. Not Piper, I mean my mom. She'd offered me a drink if I had a nightmare. I never wanted a drink; I just wanted her to hold me. I don't think I've ever felt as safe and as loved as I did in her arms."

Until now, I realized.

Here in the streetlight-lit room in Ned's old house, being held by Logan, I felt safe. I knew I should pull away. I knew I should stand on my own two feet. I'd decided that after Carey had left. And yet, I found myself snuggling closer.

Logan leaned back against the headboard and said, "Close your eyes. If you don't mind, I'll just sit here with you for a few minutes."

I should have minded, but I didn't. "Thank you," I said.

He smelled of soap. A kind of fresh, clean scent that reminded me of . . . though I realized the scents were dissimilar, I realized the smell reminded me of Piper's garden. I felt slightly amused by the realization.

And then the next thing I knew, it was morning.

Logan was still propped against the headboard, and I was still curled into the crook of his arm with my head on his chest. I could hear his heartbeat and feel the rise and fall of his chest.

I knew I should move.

I might inadvertently be Logan's roommate, but I didn't know him well enough for this.

But knowing and doing are frequently two separate things. I hadn't realized how much turmoil I was in until now . . . until I had spent a few hours in Logan's arms. All my worries and cares faded, and I simply felt safe.

Calm.

So I didn't move.

But even without moving, I felt an ache in my hip where they'd removed my bone marrow yesterday. It throbbed along to the beat of my pulse. It wasn't an agonizing pain, but it was present.

It reminded me that part of me was even now flowing through Piper. Just as part of her had always flowed through me.

I thought again of mitochondrial DNA. T. P. E.'s DNA linked us both. We had always been connected, and now we were reconnected.

And maybe, if we were lucky, we'd have years to see those connections grow and strengthen.

"You're thinking very loudly," Logan murmured, his voice scratchy from sleep. "You okay?"

I sat up and disengaged myself from Logan. "Yes, I'm fine. I'm so sorry about last night. Between the stress and the pain pill—"

"And surgery," he said.

"The surgery wasn't that big a deal." At least not compared to what Piper was going through. She'd gone through a course of heavy-duty chemotherapy. It was supposed to kill off her entire immune system, which would then be ready for the transplant. What the doctors had harvested from me would take over producing healthy white blood cells that would become her new immune system. If everything went right, she'd be cured.

But the chemo was grueling. Piper had mouth sores that were so bad that eating became a problem. And what she did manage to eat she couldn't keep down.

Ned practically lived at the hospital. I'd taken Fiona in a few times, but we didn't stay for long. Piper wasn't in any condition for guests, not even her daughters.

Having seen what she was going through, my surgery seemed like a cakewalk.

Logan obviously didn't agree. "Any time you have surgery it's a big deal," he lectured. "You were under anesthesia, and the surgery itself was invasive. I have today off until class tonight, so you are going to be waited on. Like it or not," he added with a stern expression, indicating he knew I wouldn't like it.

I snorted. "I don't need to be waited on."

Even though we'd been roommates for only a month, he'd become a friend. And I recognized the stubborn look in his eyes. It was a look that said he planned on winning this battle.

"Sometimes not really needing something but getting it anyway makes it even sweeter," he said. "I thought we'd get you set up downstairs on the couch. And I'll start a fire. It's supposed to be really cool today. You can be a lady of leisure. And because it's your day, I'll even let you pick what shows we watch."

I laughed. "I know your secret, Logan Greer. You like to pretend to be all action films and sports, but at your heart you're a sci-fi fan."

He snorted and then added, "You did mention *Firefly*. I thought we could have a marathon today."

I gingerly eased my legs over the edge of the bed and stood . . . slowly. Very, very slowly.

The throbbing turned into a sharp pain that radiated up my spine. I tried to hide it, but Logan, being Logan, noticed. "And we're going to get you some breakfast and then one of those lovely little pain pills the doctor gave you."

"It's not that bad," I told him.

"Maybe not, but it's bad enough. Siobhan, you don't have to grit your teeth and bear it. If you take it easy today, odds are you'll feel a lot better tomorrow."

I nodded. "Fine."

I made my way downstairs with the speed of someone twice my age as Logan made pancakes.

I sat at the counter and watched as he beat the eggs and then added the other ingredients. He poured the first of the batter on the griddle and brought me a cup of coffee.

"This feels like home," I said. "My dad is an awful cook. I mean, really awful. When Mom wasn't home for dinner, his specialty was creamed tuna on toast. And maybe if he could make a white sauce I could have managed it, but . . ." I shook my head.

Logan laughed and turned to flip the pancakes; then he looked at me, waiting for the rest of the story.

"The only dish Dad can make is pancakes. We had them almost every Saturday. He'd call Mom and me to the kitchen by bellowing out *Pancake Saturday.*" I smiled at the memory.

"He seemed nice when I talked to him."

Dad had wanted to come down for my procedure, but I'd convinced him that it wasn't necessary. Logan had taken his phone number and kept him posted.

"He is very nice," I said.

"You should have let him come. Sometimes the people we love need to feel needed. Last year I was home for a couple of months and stayed with Mom. I got the flu and she made me a bed on the couch, just like she used to when I was little, then she spent the day rewatching all six Star Wars movies with me. She debated about watching the originals first, or the first three episodes. I was too sick to participate in the debate, but she did fine on her own," he said with a bit of laughter.

"What did she decide?"

"One, two, three and then the older ones. I kept waking up to Wookiees and lightsabers. She still talks about it being a special day. I remind her that I'd been sick and slept through half of it. I thought she was going to tease me and say something snarky about that's what made it special, but what she said was, *That's just it. You needed me again.*"

"Maybe I should call my dad even though I talked to him yesterday is what you're saying?" I asked.

"Maybe he just wants to be needed a bit, too."

I nodded, and Logan served me a stack of pancakes. He had real maple syrup and butter.

"They're delicious," I assured him.

"Well, it's no creamed tuna," he said with a laugh.

I couldn't help but laugh as well.

Logan brought his own plate over and sat down next to me. We ate in companionable silence. After I finished about half my pancakes, he handed me a pain pill.

"I think I'll be okay without it," I said.

"I saw how you walked into the kitchen. Why don't you take this one and see how you feel by afternoon? I am a medical professional, remember?"

I smiled. "Okay."

"Follow me ma'am," he said, offering me an arm as I hobbled out to the living room. He had a pillow and a quilt laid out on the couch.

"You made me an actual bed on the couch." It would have seemed sweet no matter what, but after the story about his mom, it seemed even sweeter.

He nodded. "And I have all the *Firefly* DVDs and the movie for after."

I realized he was recreating his day with his mom, and I felt . . . I wasn't sure what I felt, but it was nice.

"Let me start the fire then clean up the kitchen before we turn them on."

I called my dad while he was in the kitchen.

He picked up on the first ring. "Ban, you okay?"

I heard the concern in his voice. "Yes. I just called to say good morning and to check in."

"How are you really? I was going to call later. I didn't want to wake you up if you were sleeping."

"I'm fine. Achy but fine. I thought maybe you and Margo would like to take a drive down to Erie this weekend. I've been helping with Fiona, but you'll love her and—"

"Honey, I can't wait to meet her. I didn't want to butt in, but these people—they're a part of you, so of course I want to meet them."

I felt tears gather in my eyes. "Thanks, Dad."

"I love you, sweetie."

"Love you, too." I collected myself and added, "I was talking about you this morning."

"Oh?" he said.

"Logan made me pancakes, and I said they were your specialty."

I could hear the smile in his voice as he said, "They still are."

"I might have mentioned creamed tuna, too," I admitted, trying to hold back the laughter.

"And of course you told him how delicious it is, right?" Dad asked.

I made a delicate gagging noise. "It's awful, Dad. Utterly awful. But I do love you."

"I know, honey. Your mom knew it, too." As if he could read my mind he added, "You've got more than enough heart to love us all."

That was my dad. He'd always known my secret worries without me having to say a thing. "I'll see you on Saturday then."

"Yes. Maybe we'll leave early so that Logan and I can make you ladies brunch."

"I'll have to see when he's working, but if not Logan, I'm sure Fiona would make brunch with you. Margo and I can manage to be waited on."

Logan came back into the living room as I hung up the phone. "Dad's coming on Saturday, if that's okay."

"I can't wait to meet him," he said.

"I wasn't sure when you were working—" I started, only to be interrupted by the doorbell.

I glanced at the clock. It was only seven thirty in the morning. Ned was getting Fiona off to school before going to the hospital. Maybe it was them?

Maybe something was wrong with Piper. My worries about not having the time I wanted with her grew like a giant balloon—expanding at a frightening speed as Logan went and got the door.

It wasn't Ned or Fiona who walked in the room. Cooper, Piper's best friend, came in with a smile. My balloon of worry popped, and I could breathe again.

"I saw the smoke and lights, so I knew someone was up. I know we've only met a couple of times, and I don't make a habit of popping in on acquaintances, but you're Piper's daughter, and you just . . ." She burst into tears and thrust a box at me. "I brought you donuts. I know, it's utterly absurd, but I wanted to do something to say thank you."

She brushed away tears and shrugged. "Like, I said, I know, it's stupid. How are you?"

"I'm fine," I said and set the box of donuts down on the coffee table.

I felt awkward with Piper's best friend. I felt as if she wanted something more from me, and I didn't know what, so I didn't know how to give it to her.

"Well, I should go." Cooper taught across the street.

"Thanks for stopping," I said awkwardly. I wasn't quite prepared when she leaned down and hugged me before she practically ran out of the house.

"You okay?" Logan asked after she left.

I nodded. "I am. It's just that . . ."

"Just that?" Logan prompted.

"I don't know what to do with that kind of emotion from people who are practically strangers. Though even as I say the words *practically strangers*, I realized that none of you are that. Not really. With my parents, and now with Margo, I'm connected and I understand the fabric of that connection. With Piper, Ned, Fiona, you, Cooper, my grandparents, and everyone else I've met here, I'm connected, but it's as if I can't understand the fabric of it. Intellectually, I get it. I'm related by blood to Piper and Fiona."

"And to your grandparents."

I nodded. "And there's an emotional connection to Ned and Cooper that's almost blood. And you?"

"Me?" he asked innocently.

"You're the biggest tangle of complicated connections that I don't understand." That was the truth. I felt as if I'd known Logan my entire life. I felt as if I could tell him anything.

I thought about how he'd held me after my nightmare. There was definitely a connection there, a complicated one.

"Me? I'm as uncomplicated as they come."

"I met you half-naked. Moved in with you that same day. You've been a friend, now a nursemaid—"

"Nurse man," he corrected, determined to put a light spin on this.

"No. Don't joke. You've become a friend. I'm not antisocial. I have plenty of acquaintances and people I am friendly with. At home, there are a number of people who wave at me as I walk by. But true friends? I only have a few. Jaylin is one."

He'd talked to her yesterday as well. "She seemed nice. She was as put out as your dad that you didn't want her here."

"That's not accurate. It wasn't that big a deal. She didn't need to throw everything in her life aside to be here."

He shrugged. I could see that he disagreed.

"She's one of the handful of people I consider a close friend. And Margo, my father's wife. And now you."

"I never thought of it, but I've got a small circle of friends, too." He shot me a smile. "You're on my list now, too."

And with that, he tucked me up in my makeshift bed, started the television, and for the next few hours I drifted in and out of medicine-induced sleep and watched my favorite space western. At one point, I remember asking Logan what he thought, and he said, "*Shiny.*"

I smiled as I drifted back to sleep.

That evening, I skipped the pain medication and simply used ibuprofen. It was enough to take the edge off, and it didn't knock me out.

Logan made me an early light dinner of soup and grilled cheese. "I'm a master of grilled cheese," he said with a laugh. After the first bite, I readily agreed. He'd made it on some kind of sourdough, whole grain bread and the cheese was melted to perfection.

He was just getting ready for work when the doorbell rang.

"Do you think Cooper's back again," I asked.

"No, not Cooper," he said in such a way that I knew he had some idea who was on the other side of the door. He hurried out of the room before I could question him.

I heard the door open, and he stepped back into the living room doorway. "I've got to go to work, so I called—"

"Me," said Piper's mother as she walked into the room. "Your grandfather's staying with Fiona, and you get me. Yes, I know, you can't believe how lucky you are."

I'd met Piper's mother a couple of times. I could do the math and realized she was easily in her seventies, but you would never know it from looking at her. She was one of those women whose body might have shrunk but whose spirit simply grew bigger to compensate. Her gray hair was cut in a short, no-nonsense style, and she had a ready smile.

I smiled back and said, "It's nice to see you, but, really, I don't need a babysitter."

"So what you're saying is that I should leave?" she asked.

Suddenly, I could see the teacher and district superintendent in Piper's mother. "No, that's not what I meant, but I'm sure Fiona needs your support—"

"Fiona and her grandfather are probably in the kitchen even as we speak, making something I would totally not approve of. Then they'll be heading with snack in hand to the living room to watch some show that I would not approve of. I never allowed television on weeknights. Though rumor has it my husband had the same covert dates with Piper when she was younger."

She smiled in such a way that I knew she'd always known about and understood her husband's rule breaking.

I nodded. "There's something special to having someone you love break the rules with you. My mom was a stickler about bedtimes, but whenever she had a meeting, Dad conveniently *forgot* to check the clock. I used to get such a kick out of that extra hour."

Piper's mother nodded. "Fiona has gone through so much that she deserves a bit of purloined pleasure when she can get it. But if I went over, they'd have to turn off the television, so it looks like you're stuck with me."

Piper had planned on me meeting her mom—my grandmother—at dinner, but she'd gotten sick and since then everything had been a whirlwind. In the weeks since I'd come to Erie, I'd met Tricia and J. P. George in passing at the hospital and at Piper's house as they helped care for Fiona. Tricia had welcomed me to the family and seemed nice enough, but we hadn't spent any real time together and certainly not time alone together.

"Go to work, Logan," Tricia said. "I'll take care of Siobhan and see to it she takes it easy." Tricia actually shooed him out of the room and took a seat. "Do you need anything?"

"No, ma'am."

Tricia George was . . . I searched for the word. Formidable. I suspected that trait had grown over time rather than diminished.

She looked me over. "I used to make Piper beds on the couch when she was young and sick."

"Logan said his mom did the same thing. Mine, too . . ." I let the sentence fade because I didn't know how she'd feel about my mom, especially having witnessed Piper's feelings over giving me up.

Piper's mom nodded as if she understood why I'd stopped talking. "Honey, we know you have parents out there. We appreciate what a wonderful job they did raising you," she said softly.

"Thank you, ma'am."

"I know we never really settled on what you should call me, but ma'am isn't it. Tricia's fine, if you like. Even Trish."

I nodded. "Okay." I didn't choose either name because my mother wouldn't have approved of me calling her by her first name. But I wasn't sure I was ready to call her Grandmother. I'd simply avoid ma'am-ing her.

I worried that she was going to pepper me with questions, but instead she said, "What are we watching?"

"Logan and I binge watched *Firefly* today. I'm open to whatever."

"Can I trust you with one of my deepest, darkest secrets?"

I nodded.

"I'm addicted to *The Secret Lives of Sissy Agave*." She took the remote and flipped with confidence to a new channel. "It's my secret vice. At home J. P. and I listen to NPR and spend a lot of quiet evenings reading. And I love it, but sometimes I need a bit of fun."

Piper's mother wasn't who I thought she'd be. I knew she was in education and so was J. P. That's one of the reasons Piper had picked Mom and Dad. She wanted to give me the gift of the same sort of childhood she'd had. But as we spent a quiet evening together, Tricia didn't pepper me with questions. She was fun and witty and didn't pressure me.

J. P. came over at eleven. "Ned's home and Fi's sleeping," he said. "You are not sleeping, young lady, and after your day yesterday, you should be." He looked like Father Christmas. Not Santa but Father Christmas. He had a quiet dignity. There was an innate sense of kindness and knowledge about him. But when he winked at me, I also saw the devilish grin.

"Was your granny making you watch all her secret television shows? The ones she doesn't think I know about?"

"Firstly, J. P., I am not now, nor have I been, anyone's *granny*. Grandma. Grandmother. Tricia. Trish. All are acceptable, but Granny?" She gave a delicate little snort. "As for television, Siobhan is the one recovering. We watched what she wanted all night."

She looked at me, and I knew she wanted me to back her up so I readily agreed, "Yes. Tricia humored me."

He snorted. "So you think you've won our Siobhan over to your subversive ways? She'll confirm your secret reality television addiction to me tomorrow when I drop by with some Frogurtz. No one can resist frozen yogurt." He winked at me.

"Don't listen to him. You don't have to sway anywhere in order to get yogurt." She leaned down and kissed my forehead. "Thank you for what you've done for Piper," she whispered. Then loudly said, "You're sure you're okay?"

"I am. But I'm so glad you spent the evening with me."

And I was. Tricia, like Piper, didn't push and prod. She wasn't trying to force a relationship but rather was present and letting it develop naturally. It made getting to know her easier.

"Well, Logan said he'd be home soon. His shift was supposed to end at eleven. He scheduled short shifts this week. Ned's next door with Fiona if you need anything, and J. P. and I can be here in ten minutes. It doesn't matter what time—you call if you need us."

I found myself tearing up. "I will call if I need you, I promise."

She nodded and they left, still playfully bickering about television shows and frozen yogurt. I had a glimpse of what I might have had if I'd known them all along. How different my life would have been if they'd always been a part of it.

I glanced at the hope chest. It still sat unopened under the window. A chest filled with Piper's hopes and dreams for me. Something tickled my cheek, and I reached up to brush it aside and realized it was a tear.

I got up gingerly and walked across the room to where the chest had sat since Logan carried it over. I finally opened it. On top there was a box. I pried the lid off it and discovered a charm bracelet. There was a little piece of paper tucked into the lid. I opened it.

Dear Amanda,

Some of the charms are self-explanatory. A car for your sixteenth birthday, a binky for your first. I made a list of each year's charm. You're turning twenty-one this year, and if I keep adding annual charms, you won't be able to wear it. So I'm adding this one last one. The small beach glass heart is for this year. I found it as I walked on Presque Isle. I thought of you as I picked it up. I took it to a local shop. They drilled the hole and added the clasp. I hope when you look at it you

111

realize that wherever I am and whatever I'm doing, I am thinking of you.

Love, Piper.

The small glass heart was easy to spot in the midst of the small gold charms. The small piece of glass had broken from something larger. A beer bottle? A soda bottle? Over time, the waves and sand had beaten and polished something that had been an accident into something beautiful. I slipped the bracelet on my wrist. It tinkled as I moved my arm.

There at the top was a leather book. It had to be the journal that Ned had mentioned and copied a page from.

I opened the cover and read the first page.

Dear Amanda,

Amanda's Pantry truly began on your fifth birthday, almost a decade ago now. I was at the grocery store buying . . . I don't remember what I was buying. Probably something with no nutritional value whatsoever. I was only twenty-one, and I didn't worry about things like proper nutrition.

I was standing in line at the register behind a young woman and a toddler. The little girl had red hair. Not auburn. Not strawberry blonde. Red. Like Orphan Annie red. Like mine. I felt a kinship with her immediately, and, of course, I thought of you.

She told how the young mother hadn't had enough money to pay for her groceries. Piper had helped her buy them and had bought the little girl a candy bar.

I had the nightmare again that night. You were cold and hungry, and I couldn't get to you. I ripped apart my pantry and couldn't find anything for you to eat. But you came into my kitchen, sat down at the counter, and picked up a candy bar that was suddenly lying there.

You looked at me and said, "Thank you," as you pushed a strand of your carrot-colored hair behind your ear and then tore into the candy.

Love,

Piper

My dream the night before had been different, but there was the same sort of feeling behind it. I got a bit of the *Twilight Zone* feeling as I read Piper's.

I suddenly realized how hard I was sobbing. I brushed at the tears and the bracelet tinkled, reminding me of its presence.

I'm not sure how long I sat there crying as I realized that T. P. E's hope chest had become Piper's hopes for me, but I was still there when Logan walked in. The lights were still on in the living room, so he came in and saw me.

He didn't say a word. He walked across the room, scooped me up—bracelet, journal, and all—and carried me upstairs to my room.

He tucked me in as if I were a small child. He brought me a glass of water and another pill. "Go to sleep," he whispered.

I heard him take a shower, and a few moments later I saw him peek into my room.

Without either of us discussing it, he came in and crawled back onto the right side of the bed he'd occupied the night before. He pulled me into his arms, and the last thing I remembered was the sound of his heart beating and the smell of soap.

Chapter Seven

"Couch," Felicity called. "Your name's funny."

"Coach," Coach Divan responded, correcting her pronunciation.

"Couch Divan. I bet people pick on you. My grandma calls her couch a divan. So you're really Couch Couch."

"Coach," he repeated.

"I like Couch better. Couch Divan. Yep. Couch Couch. Yeah, I like it—"

—*Felicity's Folly,* by Pip

I woke up to find myself in Logan's arms again sometime in the middle of the night.

The clock was on the other side of Logan, and I couldn't see over him, so I wasn't sure what time it was, but moonlight spilled through the window so it definitely wasn't morning yet.

Sharing a space with Logan—whether the house or the bed—didn't feel awkward. It felt comfortable. And maybe even familiar at this point.

He was a back sleeper. I was a side sleeper.

It felt almost normal to curl up in the crook of his arm and rest my head on his chest. Even the cadence of his heartbeat felt like a lullaby I knew by heart.

Maybe that's why I knew the moment he woke up—the tempo of his heartbeat changed.

"We have to stop meeting like this," I teased to cover my embarrassment.

In the moonlight, I could make it out as he opened his eyes slowly and offered me a long, lazy grin that stirred something in me that I hadn't expected. I saw the laughter leave his eyes and be replaced by something else as well.

Slowly, he sat up and kissed me.

It was not the comforting kiss one friend might give another. It was more. But before I could let myself fall into it, he pulled back. "We shouldn't . . ."

I scooted over to the far end of the bed. "You're right, we shouldn't. I mean, this entire situation is complicated enough. I'm sharing a house with you. We're practically strangers and . . ."

"Stop. I don't think of you as a stranger. I think of you as a friend. But there are two very valid reasons for us not to take this beyond friendship. Three maybe. You're freshly out of a long-term relationship. I don't want to be your rebound guy. Secondly, your life is in turmoil as it is."

Softly he added, "And thirdly, I'm not staying in Erie. I'm here long enough to finish my degree, but after that?" He shrugged. "I'm already signed up to go on another medical trip next summer with First Aid."

It was already October. He'd be leaving in just eight or nine months. I nodded. "My life is complex enough right now," I said. "You're right, I don't need the complications. And between school and work, neither do you."

"Friends?" he asked, extending his hand.

I shook it. "Friends."

I moved to the other side of the bed. I thought he would leave, but he didn't. He stayed on his side.

I woke and knew that it was morning even though the room was still dark. I was back in the crook of Logan's arm, and we were in the center of the bed as if some magnetic force had drawn us both from our respective sides. Part of me would have liked to stay there, but he'd warned me off last night. We were friends. I understood his reasoning.

I'd been with Carey for years. I wasn't in a hurry to rush into a new relationship after just a month.

I wouldn't take advantage of Logan's friendship again. I'd dealt with my own dreams in the past, and I'd do it again. Carey slept like the dead and never heard me, and even if he had, I wasn't sure he'd have comforted me.

I could easily go back to managing my dreams on my own.

I slipped out of bed as carefully as I could. I was still feeling an unremitting ache that was punctuated by an occasional sharp stab of pain. Still, I managed disentangling myself without disturbing Logan.

I took the journal with me and tiptoed down the stairs.

I made coffee and thought about sitting in the kitchen to drink it, but the house felt too full of Logan for me to do that.

I took my cup and Pip's journal and let myself out the back door.

I slowly made my way down the now familiar path, through the fence, and to the bench at the back of the garden.

I set the book on the bench along with my coffee cup and just sat very, very still.

I didn't pick up the journal. I'd hesitated reading it for so long. And now that I'd opened it, I wanted to gorge myself on it and read every word. Conversely, I wanted to take my time and savor these letters from Piper.

I'd felt as if reading the journal was admitting that I'd never hear the sentiments it contained from Piper herself. It felt like I was admitting defeat. But now, she'd had the treatment.

I wasn't a believer in visualization techniques—well, I guess I wasn't a nonbeliever, either. I was an agnostic about the technique. Still, I found myself picturing my bone marrow carrying suitcases and moving into Piper's blood stream. I pictured it settling in, making tiny little white blood cells. Hundreds then thousands.

The sound of Canadian geese pulled me from my absurd mental imaginings. I'd heard some people call them Canada geese, but I thought that sounded wrong, which probably meant it was right. I heard geese honking to one another, and then I saw a skein of geese in a lazy V formation heading south. One goose was out of sync, flying way to the left of the V. I wondered if he'd master the art before they hit Florida, or wherever they were going. I listened until their honking faded.

In the sudden silence, I noticed a dry, crisp smell. If Erie was anything like Port Clinton, soon the dried leaves would be covered in snow as fierce Canadian air blew off the Great Lake.

I heard a back door open, and soon Archie was running through the garden. He found me and yipped a greeting before covering me with dog kisses. He was gentle, though, as if he realized that I was still sore.

"Good morning," I told the empathetic dog. He crawled onto the bench, curled himself into a tight ball without disturbing me, the coffee, or the book, and he rested his giant head on my thigh.

I glanced at the journal. I reached over and ran the tip of my finger along its age-softened cover. Finally, I gave in and picked it up.

I turned to the second entry.

A few pages later, I had to stop for a breather. This book was going to be difficult to read because each page was filled with so much longing—so much love.

I heard the sound of a door banging and then the rustling of leaves as someone stepped on them. Even if I wasn't sitting in the garden, I'd know they were Logan's footsteps as surely as I now recognized the beat of his heart.

He came into view wearing ancient sweats, a bright orange T-shirt that proudly proclaimed, Prep, and a pair of flip-flops that were no longer in season.

He was also wearing a frown as he looked at me and said, "Siobhan, you should come in. You're still recovering."

"I can feel Piper out here, you know?" I said softly, knowing he'd understand. When I first met her she said she wanted me to see her as more than her illness. Maybe that's what I'm trying to do. At the hospital, all I see is the illness. It's as if it's so weighty that it obscures everything that's truly her.

"But here in her garden I can see her. I get glimpses of the real her. I've read a few pages of her journal, and she's there naked on the page. I wonder if the woman who planted and loved this garden, the woman who wrote me these beautiful letters, can find her way out from under that illness."

I thought of all the Pip books I'd been reading. "I can see her in her stories, too, you know? Not her illness but her heart. I can't believe how big and all-encompassing it is."

Logan nodded as if he totally understood. There wasn't much room left on the bench because Archie didn't seem inclined to move, but Logan picked up my coffee cup and squeezed into that small space. "When I was a kid, there was never a sense of shame when we went to the food pantry. Instead, there was a sense of anticipation. I knew I'd see Ms. Pip there. And when she saw me, she'd smile, and she'd ask me how I was. She'd ask about school. And when I answered, she listened as if no one else in the world mattered at that moment. Only me and my response."

I nodded. She'd been so sick since I'd been here, first just ill, then the chemo, and now the waiting to see if my bone marrow was enough.

"She made such a difference in my life," he added.

I realized we were both whispering, as if the garden deserved that kind of respect.

"She made a difference in Mom's life, too. In so many other people's lives through Amanda's Pantry or her books or reading stories to kindergarten classes or simply waving to the kids as they came and went from school."

He paused and said, "Everything she did, she did for you. Her books, the food pantry—all of it. So I guess everything I have is thanks to you. I think like Ms. Pip, Ned, and Fiona, I felt I knew you and cared about you before I ever met you. And now? It's not just the myth of Amanda that I know and care about. It's you. It's that you're here, helping when you don't have to. It's how you are with Fiona. It's how deeply you feel, just like your mom. You try to hide it, but I can see it.

"About last night, I need you to understand. It's not that I don't want to. It's that I know that I can't let my feelings go any deeper. It wouldn't be fair to either of us. You're an emotional powder keg, and I'll be gone again by this time next year.

"You asked why I called her Ms. Pip? The naming of things matters, and to me she will always be Ms. Pip because it's a mark of my respect and gratitude."

I didn't have a name for her. I called her Piper for the same reason I called her mother ma'am. They were both more to me than a first name, but for now a first name was all I had to give them.

"Names matter," I said. "I reread *Felicity's Folly*. There's a man, Coach Divan. Felicity calls him Couch Couch and sometimes Coach Couch. His name matters in the story. It made me think about Piper and what to call her. Ms. Pip is too formal, and I can't call her Mom. *Mom* is already taken. She signs all the letters I've read so far as Piper. So Piper is where I'm stuck. But I don't

119

know if that conveys everything I want. But I know what to name you—friend."

He smiled. "That's my name for you, too. Now, come in the house. I'll get you some breakfast."

I nodded and felt a little more human as I shuffled back along the path behind him. Archie followed us as far as the fence then turned and walked back toward Piper's.

The day was less blurry than the day before. I took a couple of half doses of the pain medication.

Logan didn't give me time to worry about anything. We moved on from *Firefly* to *Buffy*. I laughed loudly at how cheesy the early episodes seemed, but soon I was as totally a Scooby wannabe as Logan. He laughed when I kept asking, "How did I miss this?"

The next morning, though I wasn't ready to run a marathon, I felt more like myself, even if I was still moving slower.

I wanted to do something to thank Logan for all his care. I dug around the kitchen and found some baking mix. I had everything I needed for a mock quiche. Onions, spinach, cheese, eggs, baking mix—it took only a few minutes to mix up. I put the quiche in the oven, started the coffee, and thought about picking up Piper's journal but instead got one of her new-to-me books.

All the elements I loved about her books when I was younger were still there, but these newer stories had more . . . depth, maybe?

When I was younger, her books resonated with me because her characters felt what I felt. Now, as an adult reading them, they still resonated. Today I read *Jonah Jones and the Jupiter Smith*. Piper had written it four years ago. It was about two neighbors and classmates who were night-and-day different but were friends. Just friends. Until their senior year when Jupiter realized she might want more.

I'd never fallen in love in high school, but I remember meeting Carey. He was cute and far more social than I'd ever be. I had Jaylin as a friend and that was enough for me. But Carey knew everyone. He dragged me and Jaylin out and made us do typical college stuff. Though *Jonah and Jupiter* was written for teens, I still could relate to it—to them.

"You are a friend. A good friend. My best friend. Maybe you can be more, but I know you'll never be less than that," the book had said. I got that.

As if on cue, Logan walked in and the timer went off on the stove.

He sniffed. "What is that?"

"Breakfast," I announced triumphantly.

I got out of the chair, still a little gingerly but definitely better than I'd moved yesterday.

"You shouldn't be up and around—" he started to lecture.

I interrupted. "I'm fine. I'm still taking it easy, but I'm fine. I wanted to do something for you. You've done so much for me."

He gave a self-deprecating little snort. "No."

"Yes." I pulled the quiche from the oven.

"The coffee's hot—" I stopped short. "That was dumb. You're on your way to bed. I wasn't sure if you wanted to eat first or when you got up. This is not only easy, but it refrigerates and reheats easily. I've never had to pull an all-nighter for work. No, I take that back. Our first app. At the last minute, the customer wanted some tweaks, so we recoded for a whole night."

I smiled at the memory of coffee and ice cream. Jaylin was in love with Hershey's ice cream and kept her freezer stocked. We'd decimated her reserves.

"I'm not sure exactly what you do," he said.

"Here." I pulled out my phone and opened a small Ohio chain of grocery stores' app. "You get the hours, the week's specials. Daily specials, too, if there are any. It's got your shopper's card number in it. And there's even a spot for your shopping list."

"And you made this?" he asked.

I nodded. "Me and Jaylin. We've got a few freelancers working for us, but I think next year we're going to hire full-time help. We used to do most of the programming, but more and more we're taking care of business. But we still can do the bulk of our job at home. Maybe I get that from Piper?"

"Get what?" he asked as he dished up a hefty slice of quiche.

"Enjoying working at home, on my own."

He took a bite. "This is good."

I laughed. "Don't sound so surprised. Mom always felt everyone should be able to cook for themselves as well as have a few company-worthy dishes."

"Tell me about your parents."

I realized I'd missed talking about them. It wasn't that I thought Piper and Ned would mind any more than Dad minded me talking about them. It was simply awkward. "You'll meet Dad and Margo this weekend. Plus, you know so much about me. You've had a front row seat for my drama. So, it's your turn. I mean, I know that you wear smiley face boxers and that Piper helped your mom out. I know you travel and help people, but only in the most general way." I realized how much I wanted to know more about Logan.

He was quiet for a moment, as if searching for something he wanted to share. Finally, he nodded more to himself than to me and said, "On one of my first trips, I met a girl in Zimbabwe. I was part of a team giving inoculations. She was around two and found my skin fascinating. She told her mother I looked like a ghost."

His complexion was darker than mine. I wondered what she'd have thought of me.

"She came back two days later and brought me a white stone she'd found." He reached in his pocket and pulled out a small white stone. "She told her mom it looked like me." He ran his thumb against it and then tucked it back in his pocket.

"A couple of weeks later, there was a cholera outbreak. I was there when they brought her in." He shook his head. "She'd been so bright and funny. So full of life and potential. And then she was gone. It was such a waste. When there's an outbreak, if there's medical intervention, we can save most patients. But there are so few of us and so much need."

"And you carry the rock?"

"As a reminder. In Ms. Pip's *Terry the Terrible*, there's a line that says no one can change the world, but they can change their small corner of it. I remember her telling me the story about throwing rocks."

I nodded. "I remember you told me about that."

"So many of Ms. Pip's personal philosophies weave their way into her stories," he said as an aside. "Anyway, this rock reminds me to keep trying."

"That's a lovely sentiment. Next to Piper and you, I feel like a slacker."

Feeding the hungry, taking care of the sick—they seemed to be too good to be true. I don't think I ever did anything particularly bad, but I wasn't sure I'd ever done anything that particularly good, either. Something that made a difference.

Logan snorted. "Yeah, you're so utterly selfish. I mean, you came to Erie and just went through a major medical procedure to help someone out. Do you remember what you said to me when you were coming out of anesthesia?"

I shook my head.

"You said, 'I'd do that again.'" Logan reached out and touched my cheek, just the slightest brush of his finger against my skin. He pulled his hand back and said, "I'm thinking saving a life is considered pretty altruistic."

"How could I not help her?"

"You could have shut the door on Ned, but you didn't. So, let's just say that I think you're very much Ms. Pip's daughter. That being said, I'm off to bed. It was a long, long night." He started toward the sink as if he was ready to do the dishes.

"Nope. I'm certainly well enough to rinse a few plates. Leave them."

"You're very bossy," he said with a laugh.

"Scary. You forgot; I'm scary."

He snorted but left the dishes.

After I finished the dishes, I went back to the couch. Cooking and dishes had taken more out of me than I thought. I was not a good patient I realized. But I dozed off for a while and woke when my cell phone buzzed. Jaylin was Skyping me.

I pushed the button and smiled when I saw her. "How's business? I should be back to work next week—" I started.

"No you won't. You aren't touching a bit of work for at least another week. I read up on this. You need to take things easy, and I know you. I bet you're already plotting some way to do something." She gave me her stern-Jaylin look.

I laughed. "I might have made a quiche this morning."

She snorted in a rather Logan-esque way. "I do know you so well."

"So everything's okay?"

"Blakesley called and wants a few more *little* changes. We once again had the there's-no-such-thing-as-a-little-change-in-programing discussion, but he was adamant. I gave him an estimate on how many more billable hours he'd see because of that little change. He told me go ahead."

"I could take a look," I offered.

"Or you could lie back against that comfy-looking pillow and take a nap."

I laughed. "You are very bossy."

"Yes, I am. I didn't just call to check on you. I wanted to let you know that Carey's been calling me. He wants to know where you are."

I sighed. "He's called me, too. I finally blocked his phone number."

"Rumor has it that living with his mom's not going so hot. Poor Carey," she said without an ounce of sympathy. "You're well rid of him."

"I know. You tried to tell me, but I guess it was one of those I-had-to-figure-it-out-for-myself things."

"You're worth more than Carey, Siobhan. You deserve a man who puts you first. A good man."

As she said the words, I had a mental image of Logan.

Chapter Eight

Love just is. You can fall in love after a minute or a week or a month or years. But once you're in love, there's no taking it back, at least not if it's a true love.

—Jenny Jangle and the Frisco Kid, by Pip

On Thursday, I convinced Logan—aka my jailor—that I was indeed well enough to go to the hospital and see Piper. Granted, I was still walking as if I were twice my age. I wasn't really in pain now as much as I had an ever-present ache. I was aware of every movement. And I was ridiculously tired.

I would rather deal with pain and discomfort than the exhaustion. I was not a sit-around-doing-nothing sort of person. And though work was a lot of sitting around, I was too tired to concentrate.

I'd dressed for comfort, not style. My yoga pants, oversize sweatshirt, and Uggs wouldn't grace any fashion runway, but they were comfortable.

As we slowly entered the hospital, I really thought that a wheelchair ride to Piper's room might not be such a bad idea. But I knew Logan would simply get me in a chair and wheel me home. So I made it under my own steam.

Slowly, but I made it.

Logan had to work. I'd ridden to the hospital with him, and Tricia had said she'd give me a ride home. I might have received a brief parole from the house, but no one would hear about me driving.

"Listen, if there's any problem, you call me. I'll have my cell on me all night. And I can literally be here in minutes," Logan said. "I'll check on you if I have a break."

I nodded as I gowned up, scrubbed my hands, and added gloves and a mask. "I'll call if there's a problem, I promise. But there won't be. I'm just going to sit in Piper's room rather than sit at home."

Neither of us commented on the fact that I referred to the house we were sharing as home, but I realized that's exactly what it felt like. The house in Ohio that I'd shared with Carey seemed very distant. Like a memory.

I could almost hear the squeaky floorboard. I remembered the spot I'd dinged with the coffee table as we moved it in. But those were just memories. The house felt like a memory of a place that used to be home.

"And listen," Logan continued. "I want to be sure you understand that Ms. Pip's not going to look better today. As a matter of fact, she looks worse. That doesn't mean this isn't going to work."

I nodded again as if I understood, but as I walked into the room, I knew I hadn't really been prepared. Piper had on a rose-colored scarf this time. She was in the center of the bed and looked cadaverous. Her mouth had open sores and there were dark circles under her eyes. She had IV lines pumping her full of fluids.

Ned was sleeping in the chair next to the bed. He'd been with her almost constantly since the procedure. He startled and sat up as I entered the room.

"You shouldn't be up and about," he said by way of greeting.

"Thanks. Logan's already said as much." After I disagreed with Ned's diagnosis, I'm pretty sure the word *stubborn* was muttered

127

under his breath. When he realized I'd overheard him, he said it louder just to be sure I understood his opinion.

I looked at Ned. I knew that I looked worse for wear, but Ned looked like he should be in a bed next to Piper. "Listen, why don't you move out of that very comfortable-looking chair and go home for a bit. Visit Fiona, get a shower, maybe lie down for a nap. I'll stay here."

"You're the one who needs—"

"—to be in that chair," I said, interrupting him. Then I added, "You keep saying I'm part of the family. Well, prove it. Let me sit with Piper for a bit like a member of the family would." It was a low blow. I knew it was. But it had the desired effect.

"I'll be back later," he said, rising.

"I'll stay with her, and I swear I'll call if they need you here."

"I'm fine," Piper said, opening her eyes and speaking as if she had a mouth full of crackers. "Go see Fi."

Ned bent as if to kiss Piper; then he remembered and stood up again. "I won't be long."

"Take your time. I want to spend time with Siobhan." It was easy to see each word took effort. I knew the sores—a side effect from the drugs that had eliminated her own immune system—covered the inside of her mouth, too.

I lowered myself into the chair as, with another backward look, Ned left.

"I didn't mean to be presumptuous, but he needed a break," I said. Then I realized that more than anyone Piper needed a break, but there was no way to offer her any respite.

"How are you?" she asked.

"I'm fine." I adjusted myself in the chair, wincing a bit as I aggravated the tender site. "I know we haven't had a lot of real time to spend together, but I've been reading your journal. Every letter is like a conversation with you. I love when you tell me about what's going on in your life. And I was thinking that I wish I had something like it to give you. If I'd known, I'd have kept a journal throughout my childhood so I could give it to you now."

She offered me a small smile. "I would have liked that."

"I thought instead, I'd tell you a few stories from my childhood. I was trying to remember things I thought you'd like to know about—"

"Anything and everything," she said.

"If you lie back and close your eyes and rest, I'll do my best. I thought I'd start with Christmas when I was eight or nine."

She leaned back and closed her eyes.

I said, "Mom and Dad had a tradition. They had to go downstairs first on Christmas morning. They'd light the tree and Dad—a coffee addict—would start the pot before they called me down. I remember sitting at the top of the stairs. There was a bend in the stairway so I couldn't see anything, but I could hear Mom and Dad as they got everything ready."

I closed my own eyes. I could remember the scene. The smell of a live tree. The sound of the coffeemaker. Mom and Dad whispering, sometimes laughing.

"Then they'd call me. I tore down that year and went straight to the box with the holly wrapping paper. I'd toyed with it enough to know that it was heavy. I'd shaken it, but that didn't provide any clues."

I remembered that sense of anticipation and excitement. Mom loved to torture me with presents, so she'd wrap them and set them out early so I'd have weeks to try and guess what each box contained. That was half the fun.

This particular present had driven me crazy. "I tore into the wrapping paper and found it was full of books. They hadn't rattled because Mom had cushioned the stack with wadded-up paper. I still have all of them. Mom used to tease me about being a book hoarder." I added the point of this particular memory. "There was one of yours there."

"Which one?"

"*Belinda Mae's Very Bad Year.*"

She smiled and nodded.

"I loved the series. I enjoyed that you aged Belinda Mae in the stories. I wish I could say I read that one first, but there was a three-volume collection of Nancy Drew books. I'd read all the Trixie Beldens, and Mom had found another teenage sleuth to pick up my reading slack. I was convinced I was going to be a world-famous detective someday."

I'd thought I'd travel the world, solving mysteries like Trixie. Instead, I worked from home like Piper. And I didn't mind being a homebody at all. I thought again about my house in Port Clinton, and I realized again that it no longer felt like home.

"I opened that Nancy Drew book and started reading. I only stopped when Mom said it was time for breakfast. And by dinner, I'd read the first book and half of the second. After we finished, Dad casually asked if I wanted to finish opening my presents. That's when I realized that after that first box, I hadn't opened any of the rest of my presents."

Piper smiled at my story. "They sound wonderful."

"They were. I read the journal entry where you talk about starting Amanda's Pantry. I wanted you to know I was never hungry and I was always loved.

"I'm still sorting out everything—all my feelings—but I do know that giving me up hurt you. I also know you wanted to give me a happy childhood, and you did that. And though it's taken me some time to get here, I wanted to say I'm glad I'm here. I'm glad I'm getting to spend time with you, Fiona, and Ned."

"I'm so glad," she said thickly. "Tell me another story?"

I hadn't thought of a second story, but I immediately knew which one to tell. "I was the last girl in my class to need a bra. Not that I didn't make Mom buy me some. But it was like putting a pebble in a slingshot . . ."

I continued regaling her with stories from my childhood. And I watched as she fought against falling asleep. I finally said, "It's okay. I'll come back tomorrow, and I'll think of some more stories for you. I'll ask Dad to come up with some, too."

When the nurse came to ask me to give them some privacy, I tore off the gown and gloves, picked up my things, and walked down the hall looking for someplace to hide. We'd passed a chapel on the way in, so that's where I headed.

I sank onto a seat and stared at nothing as I thought about Piper's journal and my attempt to give her a taste of the same through my silly stories.

I knew I hadn't come close, because while Piper had shared stories, she'd actually shared so much more. It was as if she had opened a vein on every page of that journal and let raw emotions bleed out.

I'd given her stories but not that emotional wallop.

I ran my finger across the cover of the journal. I'm not sure why I'd tucked it in my purse when we'd come, but I had.

I was about halfway through reading it. I was taking it slowly because I knew I'd never read it for the first time again. I opened the journal and reread a piece of today's entry.

I don't want this journal to come off as if I regret giving you up for adoption. I don't. But knowing I did the right thing doesn't mean I forgot about you. I miss you. I know, it's odd to hear that someone you've never met misses you, but I do. You're a constant in my life. You've influenced so many of my choices. I believe I'm a better

person because of you. And that's a gift from you to me.
A gift I want to thank you for.

I felt tears fill my eyes. She'd missed me.

My life had been full of love and family, and though I'd always known I was adopted, and occasionally my birth parents crossed my mind, I didn't think of her often.

I wiped at my eyes and tried so sniff back more tears.

Someone asked, "Are you all right?"

I turned around and saw a woman who was about my age looking at me with concern. She had dark hair and a pale complexion. In another time, they might have said she had porcelain skin.

I found myself nodding that I was okay to her, but we both knew it for the lie it was. She was kind enough not to call me on the fib, though. She simply said, "Okay, then." She started to sink back in her seat.

I could have turned around and gone back to my brooding, but instead I found myself asking, "How do you miss someone you hardly know?"

I didn't expect her to have an answer for me. So I wasn't surprised when she said, "I'm not sure."

"I don't know her. My mother. My birth mother. And he said—her husband—he said that they'd been waiting for me. I believed him, but I thought it was waiting like waiting for your vacation or even like a kid who's waiting for Christmas. I thought she was looking forward to meeting me someday. But that's not it. She wrote this—" I held out Piper's journal. "And when I read it, I can feel her *aching*. That's the word. She was *aching* with the waiting."

As I clutched the locket, I was aware of the bracelet slipping toward my elbow. "I occasionally thought about finding her, you know. But I put it off. I knew I'd look for her someday, but life got in the way. And she was out here waiting for me. Aching."

The woman nodded, as if she understood my word vomit. She confessed, "I thought earlier that maybe the word *waiting* comes from the word *weight*. I thought I'd be crushed under the weight of my waiting."

I nodded and pushed at my hair, which seemed to have a mind of its own tonight. "Yes. I can feel her aching under the weight of it on every page. Now the tables are turned and I'm the one who's waiting, aching under the weight of it all."

"This is not a normal conversation for two strangers." She offered me a rueful smile. "I think that everyone here who's waiting has a common bond. It means none of us are strangers, even if we've never met before. I'm Addie."

"I'm Siobhan. Who are you waiting for?" I asked her gently.

She hesitated a split second before saying, "My husband. He had heart surgery today. They kicked me out of ICU and told me to go home for the night, but I can't."

"My . . . I don't know what to call her. Mother isn't right. I had a mother who loved me and raised me. A mother I adored. But birth mother seems too formal. Everyone else calls her Piper or Pip, but she's more than that to me." I kept circling back to what to call Piper. Of all the things that were going on in my life, I wasn't sure that was the most important thing, and yet it was a point I kept coming back to.

"Maybe giving her a name doesn't matter. It's hard to watch someone you love suffering."

"I've only just met her. How can I love her? How can I love any of them?" I asked.

"Sometimes love comes quickly, sometimes more slowly. Real love comes in its own time," she said.

133

It reminded me of something Piper had written in *Jenny Jangle and the Frisco Kid*. "Love just is. You can fall in love after a minute or a week or a month or years. But once you love, there's no taking it back, at least not if it's a true love."

Rereading her children's books as an adult had shown me that Piper had hidden some beautiful gems in her fiction. Not just her way with words, but the sentiments behind them.

I nodded. "She always loved me. It's on every page. Every single one of them. She built a life around me and loved me. Every day of my life, she loved me so much. How could I not have felt it? Even not knowing her, how can someone be loved that much and not be aware of it?"

Addie shook her head. "I don't know. You're right; it seems as if that kind of love should be palpable. And maybe if someone loves you that much, it's hard not to love them in return."

Suddenly Logan was in the door. "Siobhan?"

"Logan, is she okay?" I asked.

"She's fine."

I stood up, clutching Piper's journal. I turned to Addie. "I hope your husband's okay."

She took my hand and squeezed it. "I hope *she* is as well."

I noticed that she didn't give Piper a name. I smiled my thanks as I followed Logan back into the hall. He looked as if he belonged here, with his scrubs and stethoscope wrapped around his neck. "They're done with Ms. Pip and said you're welcome to come back in."

"They called you?" I asked.

"I stopped in to check on you," he admitted.

I laughed. "Thanks, *Mom*."

We both realized what I said, but neither of us mentioned it. Instead, Logan said, "Ban, *motherly* is not the word I'd use to describe how I feel about you." And then, standing in a hospital hallway, he leaned down and kissed me. It was tender, but he was right, not the least bit motherly.

Neither of us mentioned the kiss or the talk we had about not pursuing anything more than friendship. Nor did I ask for a more specific description of his feelings. He walked me back to Piper's room, where I scrubbed, gloved, and gowned back up before I let myself back into her room.

She was sleeping, which meant I had nothing to do but sit in the quiet room and think as I looked out the window at all the cars driving by. Snippets from my talk with Addie and from Pip's books and journal wove their way through my thoughts.

You're a constant in my life.

The weight of waiting.

A gift.

And as my fingers brushed my lips and I thought about Logan, *Love just is.*

As I watched the lights of cars pass outside the window, I mixed the words like a game of Magnetic Poetry.

Weight is waiting for a gift.

Love just is a constant.

I looked at Piper. She looked pale and gaunt. Her skin seemed to be stretched over bones, as if that's all that was left of her, skin and bones.

Her breathing hitched.

I turned back to the window. It was easier. Easier than worrying what would happen next. Easier than wondering if she'd ever leave this hospital room. Easier than praying I was enough to cure her.

I plucked words from all my worries and made another Magnetic Poetry sentence in my head.

Easier than worrying.

Praying a cure.

I sensed Piper was awake before I turned.

"What were you thinking?" she asked.

"Do you remember those Magnetic Poetry games? So many thoughts keep whizzing past. I was grabbing words from all of them and rearranging them in my head like that."

She nodded.

"I'm worried about you and wondering what happens next." I didn't say it, but I worried she'd never leave this hospital room.

"You worry too much," she whispered.

"You've given me a lot to worry about."

As if sensing what I was thinking, she said, "I could leave the hospital and get hit by a bus."

"What?" I asked.

"You've got to stop worrying. I think we all have a choice. We can live worrying about what happens next. We can make all the plans we want, but eventually we have to admit we have no control. Once you realize that, it's easier to live in the present. And my present is very good. You're here with me. I choose to concentrate on that."

"I loved your books when I was young. You seemed to understand the things I was feeling. And now that I've met you in person? Not only do you have empathy, you have a way with words. You're able to put your feelings into words. You're able to put *my* feelings into words."

"I'm no Shakespeare, but I do love telling stories. But right now, I want to hear a story. So tell me another one until Ned comes back."

I nodded. "When I was still in grade school, a neighbor lent me a copy of Zenna Henderson's *The People*. Have you ever read it?"

Piper shook her head without opening her eyes.

"They were aliens who looked human but who had power. They were stranded here on Earth. Some of their people got lost.

I wondered if I was one of them. For weeks I tried to move things with my mind or hear other people's thoughts. I finally had to admit there was a very good possibility that I was human, not alien." I laughed.

Piper didn't. Tears leaked out from beneath her closed eyes.

"Hey, I didn't tell you that to make you sad. I told you because meeting you was a relief. I mean, having magic mind powers might be cool, but I think being straight-up human, with all our foibles and intricacies, is even more wonderful. But best of all, knowing that I'm related to you is a treasure. I love your . . ." I tried to come up with the right words. "World view. I'm not sure if that's exactly right, but I can see it in your books, in your journal, and even in our conversation tonight. I love how you see the world. You see the best in everyone. Logan told me what you did for him and his mom. You helped shape his life. Hers, too."

"When I get out of here . . ."

"You will avoid busses at all cost," I teased.

Piper laughed, which had been my intent. "Now if you lie back and close your eyes, I'll tell you one more story before I go."

"Yes, ma'am." Piper sank back in the bed, and I tried to ignore how small she looked against the stark white sheets.

"When I was maybe ten, my neighbors and I built a tree house near a local creek. It probably has a real name, but to us it was just Salamander Creek because there—"

"There were so many salamanders?"

"I don't know about so many. We only ever caught one. But we imagined there were more," I assured her most solemnly.

She laughed again.

Maybe I couldn't do much for her. But I could do this. I could give her stories from my youth and try to fill in all those missing years for her.

The next morning, I woke up curled against Logan. It was becoming a familiar start to my days. I lifted my head and studied him as he slept. The sound of his breathing wasn't quite a snore, but it was louder than his waking breathing.

By all measures, I'd known him such a short time. A moment. But he didn't feel like an acquaintance or even a new friend. I knew him more intimately than I'd ever known anyone, even Carey who I had been with for eight years. Maybe not all the biographical things, but I felt as if I knew *him*, the inner parts that made him so amazing.

How had I gotten so tangled up with Logan so quickly? Was it simply that circumstance had thrown us together or could it be something more?

"You are the loudest-thinking woman I've ever met," he said without opening his eyes.

"Logan," I started, but I couldn't think of what else to say. I knew he was teasing and expected me to tease him in return. He was waiting for me to make some sassy or snarky response. But I couldn't seem to find my usual casual quips.

When my silence went on too long, he slowly opened his eyes and looked at me. I saw as understanding filled them. Without a word, he pulled me into his arms. This was no friendly or comforting embrace. It was simply *more*.

And I didn't just want *more*, I needed it.

Neither of us spoke as my familiarity with Logan moved to a new, unexplored intimacy. He was gentle, probably worried about my surgery.

And the feelings for Logan that had been changing became even more.

Chapter Nine

"I hate it when Auggie calls me Julie. I keep telling him that everyone calls me Jules, but he doesn't listen."

Her grandma nodded. "Julie is your name."

"I know, but I didn't pick it. Your daughter did. Jules is the name I picked."

"See if you can pick out this knot." Her grandmother handed her a horrible mess of yarn. After a few minutes of fuming and picking, Jules admitted defeat. "It's totally tangled."

"It happens," her grandmother said. "Strings, like thoughts and feelings, can get tangled without us even being aware it's happening. And before you know it, they're in a knot that can't be undone."

"We're talking about Auggie now, not the yarn, right?" Jules asked.

Her grandmother's laughter was her only response.

—Julie and Auggie, by Pip

I held Piper's book.

I knew that Piper's friend Cooper was really named Julie. I imagined she went by Cooper for very much the same reason as Julie in the book went by Jules. I wondered how many little tidbits from Piper's real life were buried in the pages of her fiction like

139

Easter Eggs in movies—those little hidden tidbits that directors buried in so many films.

I ran my fingers over the cover. I'd picked up this book to reread one particular section. I flipped to the page I'd dog-eared.

"Strings, like thoughts and feelings, can get tangled without us even being aware it's happening. And before you know it, they're in a knot that can't be undone."

That's how I felt. As if my feelings, like my thoughts, were a tangled mess.

I'd left my bed before Logan woke up, hoping to sort everything out before I saw him. We'd both talked about all the reasons why we shouldn't move our relationship beyond the bounds of friendship. But I don't think either of us had really tried to find reasons why we should.

"Penny for your thoughts," he said, handing me a cup of coffee as he sat on the bench next to me.

"How did you find me?"

"Siobhan, you are not that complex," he said with a grin. "It was an easy guess."

I laughed and took a sip of my coffee.

"Should we talk about last night?" he asked.

"There's not much to be said, is there? I was just thinking about one of Piper's books, *Julie and Auggie*." I handed him the copy.

"Here." I pointed to the passage. "That describes everything about me right now. I'm a knotted ball of string. But there's one small section that's emerged from the tangle. You. I know you'll be gone next summer, but, frankly, I'll be gone even sooner. I've been in Erie longer than I ever intended, and I'm staying awhile yet, just to make sure Piper's okay. But someday soon, I'll go back to my old life. And I understand you have a life planned. But right now, we're both here. I don't regret last night. As a matter of fact, I plan to repeat it, if you're willing. No strings for either of us."

He slid closer, his thigh pressed against mine, and smiled. "I've become accustomed to waking up with you in my arms."

"That's good because I've become accustomed to your snoring."

"I don't snore," he protested.

I was far more comfortable bantering with Logan than trying to delve deeper into what this new aspect of our friendship meant. I grabbed on to the snoring debate. "Not an all-out snore, but there's definitely some very loud breathing going on. A couple more years down the pike, and it'll be a full-blown snore."

He wrapped his arm around me gingerly, so I wouldn't spill my coffee, and we sat quietly in Piper's garden, watching the leaves rain down from the trees.

Everything was a tangle, but I was right, the Logan string wasn't. Whatever we had right now was right.

"Hey, Ban, your dad's here," Fiona called from somewhere at the front of the garden.

"He's early," I said, disentangling myself from Logan.

"He's anxious to see you for himself," Logan said. And then he kissed me tenderly. "I know the feeling," he said then looked at me.

"We're good," I assured him. He nodded, and we hurried along the garden path to the gate.

"You're here," I called as I spotted my dad. I ran out to greet them. Well, run might be too generous a description for my speed. Faster-than-I-was-the-day-before walk with a slight hitch was probably closer.

My dad wrapped me in his arms but hugged me gently. "I am. I couldn't stay away another minute. I'm really trying to give you some space to figure everything out, but . . ."

"I needed you, and you came," I said, my voice muffled against his chest.

He tightened the hug.

When we finally separated, I turned to say hi to Margo, who was already talking to Logan.

"Margo, I can see you don't need introductions, but Logan, this is my dad, Patrick. Dad, Logan Greer."

They shook hands, and Dad said, "So you're my daughter's unexpected roommate."

"I am. I'm not around a lot. I mean between school and work I basically eat and sleep here."

Speaking of where Logan slept made my cheeks feel warm. My father noticed and raised an eyebrow but didn't say anything. "I wanted to talk to Siobhan for a few minutes if you don't mind."

Logan nodded his understanding. "Margo, I don't have to leave for work for an hour or so. Would you like a tour of the house?"

"Yes," she said, patting my shoulder. "I'm so glad you're okay."

Dad's new wife really was a sweet lady. "Thanks, Margo. It wasn't a big deal."

Logan made a face from behind Margo's back. I didn't need words to know he was scolding me for underplaying the surgery.

I ignored his silent rebuke and turned to my dad. "Why don't I show you Piper's garden?"

Dad nodded.

As we walked past Logan and Margo, my father's hand brushed hers, as if he couldn't resist the urge to make contact with her.

I never doubted that he loved my mother, but I was equally sure he loved Margo.

"I'm glad you found her," I said as we walked into Piper's garden.

"I am, too," he said as we stepped through the gate. "Wow."

"Yeah, it's pretty magnificent, isn't it? Even in the fall as everything is dying off, you can't miss what a special place it is." I led him to the bench I'd just left. I pointed out a few of the plants I recognized now. "Fiona's been teaching me about plants and birds. She's better at the birds than the plants. Sometimes she points out something, gives me a long lecture about it, and then starts giggling because I bought into her fiction. I think there's a chance she's a born storyteller like Piper."

"I want to meet her," Dad said.

"She called to let me know you were here, so I'm pretty sure she'll be out sooner rather than later." He looked nervous and ill at ease, and I was pretty sure it didn't have anything to do with meeting Fiona. "What did you need to say to me, Dad?"

I could see it, his need to tell me something. It was something he didn't think I'd like. I felt a spurt of fear. What if he were sick?

"Are you okay? Are you sick?" I asked.

From his expression, I knew he was all right. "No, honey, it's not that. I planned to tell you sooner, but there was Ned's visit and Carey, and then you came here. I didn't want to tell you on the phone and—"

"Dad, you're killing me," I said. Not knowing was worse than knowing.

"Margo and I are moving to Atlanta," he finally said, interrupting my musings.

I let out a long breath. "Okay. Why?"

He looked like a kid who was being sent to the principal's office. "I was offered a position there. It's too good to pass up."

"That's wonderful, Dad," I said as I hugged him again. He wasn't sick. My relief spread over me like a blanket. My dad was okay.

"Seriously, don't do that to me again. Why were you so nervous?"

"Because this is not a good time for you," he said. "So many things are changing. Carey. Piper. All of it. I want to be here for you, but I'll be gone. We're planning on moving over the holiday break. We put the house on the market last week. I feel as if I'm deserting you."

"Dad, I would never think that." When Dad and Margo moved in together, he'd lived at her place for a year before he'd sold my childhood home, and they bought a house together when they married. "I'm happy for you."

"But I'm worried about you."

The fact he was worried made me feel loved. "Dad, do you remember my senior year when I got so nervous about going to college? I'd always known exactly who I was and what I wanted in high school. But I'd achieved those goals, and I was moving away from you and Mom, moving into a dorm with a total stranger. I was terrified. I'd had to put undeclared down for a major because I didn't have a clue what I wanted to do. And you said . . . ," I prompted.

"I have no idea," he said. "But I'm sure it was wise and sage and all that," he added with a grin.

"The only constant is change."

"Well, it was wise, but it's not original," he said with a laugh.

"Ah, but you added something more original. You said no matter what you do, things change. You can curse those changes or embrace them. Well, I embraced them. I met Jaylin. And here I am, with a career I'd never dreamed of and a happy life. Even this—Piper, Ned, and Fiona—is more than I ever could have imagined. I didn't know what to expect, but, Dad, they're truly wonderful. I'm happy I've met them."

"And Logan?" he asked with that all-knowing dad look I think he took a class on perfecting—a class he'd aced.

"He's been a good friend." I thought about how Logan held me at night. No judgments or trying to put moves on me. He'd simply been there for me. "A very good friend."

Dad didn't say anything. He just shot me another of his classic looks.

"That's it, Dad."

He *humphed* me.

"Back to your move. You don't have to worry about me. And while we're both adults, you have my blessing if that's what you wanted."

He laughed. "Maybe it is. The university is putting us up until we find a place. We'll be looking for a house with guest rooms so whenever you come for a visit you'll have someplace to sleep. And we'll be close enough for you to go see Jaylin. It's only a few hours down to her place. No more winters and . . ."

I listened to him talk enthusiastically about his plans, but I could still hear his concern for me. I reached out and took his hand. "Dad, the only constant is change. I'll be fine."

"I know you just had surgery and that this isn't the best time, but I'm afraid there is no best time, and I didn't want to have you find out some other way."

I kissed his cheek. "Thank you for worrying. I—"

"Ban," Fiona called.

A split second later, Archie barreled down the path and barked at my dad once then went to kiss him. Archie was definitely not a good guard dog.

"I'm back here," I called. I turned to my dad. "I told you. Batten down the hatches. You're about to face a tsunami."

Seconds later, Fiona came down the path as I was petting Archie's head.

"I gave you a few minutes," she said to me. "Dad said to be polite, so I was, but I couldn't wait any longer." She turned to my dad. "I'm her sister. I'm not sure what that makes you to me. My sister's dad? They don't have a name for that, and Mr. Ahearn sounds weird. I mean, if my sister's calling you Dad and I call you Mr. Ahearn—"

"What about an honorary uncle?" I suggested.

Dad smiled. "I'd like that."

"Me, too," Fiona said. "I don't have any aunts and uncles, so I could use one. Uncle . . ."

She waited for his name.

"Pat," he supplied.

"Pat. Uncle Pat. Yeah, that works."

"Are you going to give him lessons on how to be an uncle?" I asked, then turned to my father. "The first day, Fiona told me what was required from sisters."

Fiona's hair was in a loose ponytail, so as she nodded, strands of hair started flying out of it. "I told Ban that she had to always think I'm right and that I'm perfect. I think that applies to ornery uncles, too."

"Honorary," I corrected. "Dad's many things but ornery isn't one of them."

I could see my father was thoroughly charmed. "I'm pretty sure that thinking that you're perfect is not going to be a problem."

"I know, right?" Fiona teased.

"My stepmother's in the house with Logan. If Dad's your honorary uncle, that makes Margo an honorary aunt. And I've heard tell she's very good at spoiling nieces."

"Yeah? I better go meet her." She took two steps toward the hole in the fence and then turned back around and hugged my dad, who was caught unaware but adjusted to an armful of nine-year-old just fine.

When Fiona released him, she said, "I thought about it and I gotta say thank you to you. I know Mom would say it if she were here. You were a good dad to my sister. I know that's all Mom ever wanted."

I was still blinking back tears as she shot through the hole in the fence.

I noticed Dad was blinking hard as well. "She's something," he said. "You tried to explain it to me, but I don't think kids like Fiona can adequately be described. They need to be experienced."

"Ned's heading into the hospital soon, so if you don't mind, you'll have the day to experience Fiona in her fullest. But come on; let me introduce you before he takes off."

We walked back up the path, Archie at our heels.

Though I now felt at home here, I knocked on the back door today. It felt cheeky to just invite guests in.

Ned came to the door and smiled. "Mr. Ahearn. I'm so glad you got here before I left." He held the door open, and as we entered he extended his hand.

"Ned, I'm Pat," Dad said, shaking Ned's hand.

"Logan just texted that we should all head over that way. He made breakfast before he had to leave for work." Ned turned to Dad. "Siobhan and Logan have taken turns seeing to it that I'm fed and that there's always someone here for Fi. You raised a wonderful daughter."

I realized that Ned was worried about stepping on my dad's toes. But Dad smiled and nodded. "We did okay."

"I'm right here, you two."

Dad ignored me and still grinning at Ned, said, "I'm sure you can appreciate how hard it was dealing with someone like Siobhan. I mean, a straight A student who never gave us any grief. Arduous is the word I'd use to describe the experience."

They walked back outside and over toward our house, joking as if they'd known each other for years. Of course, I was the butt of their jokes, but I didn't mind. It was great to see them getting along.

And I was right; Margo was quite willing to play Fiona's surrogate aunt.

Breakfast was a wonderful affair. The only way it could have been better was if Piper had been there, too.

An hour later, Ned stood up. "I need to head to the hospital. You're sure you're okay with Fi today?"

"Dad, I'm an utter delight," Fiona proclaimed. "Of course Ban is okay with me. And Uncle Pat and Aunt Margo are already marveling at how lucky they are to have me in their lives."

Margo and Dad laughed at Fiona's proclamation and assured Ned as well.

I walked Ned to the front door. "Let me know how she's doing," I said. Most days he sent out a text after the doctor came around.

"Definitely," Ned promised. "She's going to want to meet them."

"If she's up to it, that's great. If not, she'll meet them soon."

Ned kissed my cheek. It surprised me. Over the last weeks, we'd built a solid foundation for a relationship, but to date it hadn't included any kissing. I smiled at him. "What was that for?"

"That was because . . . just because."

I kissed his cheek in return. "I just-because you, too," I assured him.

I watched as he walked back to his driveway and got in his car before I went back inside.

A half hour later, Logan got ready to leave. He called his good-byes, and I left the backyard, where Dad, Margo, and Fiona were playing with Archie, and walked Logan out. "Thanks for making breakfast," I said.

"Anytime. I'll see you tonight."

I watched as he pulled away from the house. I was right. My life might still be tangled, but the Logan string was looking fine.

It was a lovely day. Fiona decided she was Dad and Margo's tour guide. We went to the peninsula and took a walk down the beach. The lifeguards had long since hung up their whistles for the season, and the beaches were pretty deserted. But Fiona pointed out various birds and found more beach glass.

After lunch, Ned called.

I will confess, I was nervous about this meeting. Not that I thought Dad and Piper wouldn't like each other. I wasn't sure why, to be honest, but I was.

Margo and Fiona stopped at the gift shop as we entered, so just Dad and I went to Piper's room. We put on the gowns and masks and went inside. "Dad, this is Piper. Piper, my father, Pat Ahearn."

Piper managed to say hello before she broke into tears. After a moment, she pulled herself together and said, "I feel as if I'm meeting an old friend after our e-mails. Thank you, Pat. You don't know how much it means. Thank you."

"What e-mail?" I asked.

Dad looked embarrassed. "You mentioned you were coming in and telling Piper some of your childhood stories. And Margo and I started packing, so when I found your mother's memory box, I started scanning things and sent a bunch of them to Piper. Logan gave me her e-mail address."

"Old report cards, pictures you drew, snapshots of you," Piper explained. "And a few anecdotes."

"Dad." I hugged him. "Thank you."

"Your mom and I used to joke that friends must have gotten tired of us bragging about you. It's nice to have an audience who hangs on your every word and story. Someone who agrees that you are as amazing as your mom and I always knew you were."

Listening to Dad and Piper talk, I realized the only things I needed to be embarrassed about were the stories he was sharing.

". . . and she got home at ten. I could hear them on the porch, and when she didn't come in, I looked out the window to check and—"

"Dad," I said, knowing where this story was going and hoping he'd stop but knowing he wouldn't.

I was right. He had no intention of stopping.

"—just in time to see her smack Johnny in the face and tell him that a kiss good night was one thing, but grabbing her butt was just rude."

"It was," I maintained, laughing along with them.

After a half hour, Piper was starting to droop, and Dad spotted it as easily as I did. He said, "We need to be going, but it was so nice to finally meet you in person, Piper. Thank you."

No one asked what he was thanking her for. And when Piper said, "Thank you," no one asked about that, either.

Chapter Ten

"You're my friend," Brenda said.

"And you're mine," Craig agreed.

"But what if . . ." She didn't say anything more because she didn't know what to say or how to say it.

But Craig, as always, understood. He nodded and said, "Yes. What if?"

—*The Naming of Things,* by Pip

I woke up with a start. For a moment, I wasn't sure where I was, but I heard Logan's presnore and felt his arm between my head and the pillow. I was still, in hopes that I wouldn't disturb him. I hadn't needed comforting last night, and yet he was here.

After my dad and Piper met a week and a half ago, a lot of my tangled emotions had unknotted. Dad was right, loving Piper, Ned, and Fiona didn't make me love him or Margo any less. It didn't make me love my mom any less. My heart had stretched and was comfortable with its new dimensions. Everyone I loved fit very nicely within it.

I turned my head slightly. I could see Logan in the early morning light. The shadows couldn't obscure the view of a man I'd come to know so well. I saw him. I really *saw* him in a way I doubted he'd be comfortable with.

151

He was a man who didn't want to be committed to anyone. He was a will-o'-the-wisp who'd stopped here for but a moment. Soon he would move on to someplace else. He was a man of infinite kindness and compassion, not only for the people he'd helped all over the world, but for me as well. He'd welcomed me and stood by me. He was smart and sexy.

He was everything Carey had never been. He was everything Carey never could be.

When I looked at my newly expanded heart, I could feel him there along with everyone else.

He'd made his priorities clear from the start. I knew he liked me and thought of me as a friend. I knew he cared for me. And I knew he'd be gone next summer.

If I had studied psychiatry, maybe I'd have theories on why he never stayed in any one place for long. Maybe all those years when his mom—and he by proxy—had struggled and never had a home had left their mark. Maybe that was mixed with his effort to be like Piper—to toss his stones in the ocean and make his ripples.

Maybe it was simply something inherent in him—a need to go to new places and try new things.

Whatever the combination of reasons, I wouldn't try to change him. I would never try to make him be something other than what he was.

"Siobhan?" he said, a question tied up in just my name. "You're thinking very loudly again," he said in what had become his morning greeting.

"I was thinking it's got to be after eight. I need to get out of bed." I slipped out from between the covers and kissed his forehead. "Go back to sleep. You didn't come up to bed until after one."

"I might just doze for a few more minutes. Unless you want to come back in bed and join me? We could probably think of something—"

"Ban," Fiona screamed from downstairs. "Ban."

I smiled at him. "I was tempted, but it looks like my day's starting early." I shrugged on a sweatshirt as I hurried down the stairs barefoot.

Fiona was dressed for school, but her hair was in a very sloppy-looking ponytail.

"Hey, munchkin. Did you want me to braid—"

"Nah. Mom called Dad. The doctor came by early. He said her white cell numbers are climbing."

"You're sure?" After a bone marrow transplant, the doctors watch for signs that it's working. The biggest sign is when the white blood cell numbers start to climb. It meant they were working. They call it engraftment.

Engraftment. We'd been waiting for it.

"Yep." Fiona let out a yelp, as if all her joy needed someplace to escape to, like a pressure valve, or the whistle of a teapot.

I hollered a happy yelp of my own.

The two of us were dancing around the kitchen like loons when Logan came down barefoot with just a pair of sweats on. He slipped his T-shirt on as he asked, "What's up?"

"Engraftment, baby," I said and pulled him down the last couple of stairs to join me and Fiona.

"Dad's on his way in to see her after he drops me off."

"Tell him I'll stop in later."

Fiona hugged me. "Thank you," then she ran out the back door and through the hole in the fence.

"What time do you have to leave today?" I asked Logan.

"Eleven."

"Good."

I flung myself into his arms, and after a long, slow kiss, I took his hand and led him back upstairs.

When Logan left, I drove to the hospital with him.

I was practically walking on air as I made my way up to Piper's room. The route was familiar now.

I scrubbed my hands, still changed into a gown, and still put on a mask and gloves. But engraftment meant someday soon I wouldn't have to do that.

Someday soon I could walk up to Piper and hug her with no precautions or worries.

"Good morning, sunshine," she said from her bed. Ned was sitting next to her in the chair and smiled as well.

Maybe it was my imagination, but I thought she had more color in her cheeks. If I was imaging it, it was okay because she'd have the color for real soon.

"I'm so happy," I said.

"I am, too," she said.

"Does that mean I'm out of the doghouse?" Ned asked. He was teasing.

"What are you in the doghouse for?" I asked as I pulled up another chair.

"Oh, I've been there ever since you came to the house and Piper found out I went to see you."

"It's not that I'm not happy you came, but like I said the first day, I didn't want to guilt you into it. But yes, Ned, you're out of the doghouse."

"Piper, Ned . . ." I tried to figure out how to say what I needed to say. I finally settled on how. "Okay, here's today's story for you, Piper."

She sank back against her pillow and smiled. Ned started to stand, but I said, "No. It's for you, too."

He sat back down.

"When I went away to college, I had a rough time of it the first few weeks. I wasn't sure where I fit there. In high school, I'd had a goal in mind. Graduate with a high GPA and get into the school of my choice, OSU. I did that, and suddenly I didn't know what I wanted next. I was kind of lost. But I checked into my dorm and met my roommate, Jaylin. She was nerdy and beautiful, though she's never realized she is. She's always a bit mystified when a guy hits on her. She always rebuffs those kinds of advances because she says if a guy just likes her because of the way she looks, that says a lot about him, and what it says is enough to convince her she's not interested.

"Anyway, I moved in with her. She dragged me out to campus activities. Plays, movie nights, mixers. I'd complain and say I didn't want to go, but she'd ignore me and soon I'd be out at one event or another, and I'd have fun. And then next time, she'd drag me along again, and I'd have fun. And soon, I forgot that I didn't know where I belonged. I started discovering a few activities and taking her. She gave me a push, and I landed exactly where I was supposed to be, and I was happy to be there."

I wasn't sure the analogy was working, so I said, "That's what happened when Ned showed up at my door. I'd thought of you. And I frequently thought I should go look for you. But it was like when I started college. There were too many possibilities, and they were all overwhelming. When I went to school, I was leaving my parents and I knew it was hard, especially on Mom. We'd been so close. But we talked on the phone every day and she got busy with a new school year. By the time I came home for Thanksgiving, we'd all adjusted to the change. My home was still with them, but I was at home at school, too. I couldn't imagine my life without Jaylin and classes and Carey."

Yes. Carey had been an important part of my growing up. He'd been far more social than even Jaylin.

"After I graduated, Jaylin and I lived in a crappy apartment and started the company. She eventually moved to North Carolina with her boyfriend, and I bought the house and Carey moved in. And I had a new home. So did Jaylin, but she was still a big part of my life."

I knew I wasn't telling this with the ease that Piper would have. But I'd finally wound my way to the point of today's story.

"It was like that with you. And now that I've found you, well I can't imagine my life without you in it. Ned, I've never said it but thank you. Thanks for not listening to Piper and coming to get me."

I looked at Piper. "I obviously am better at programming than telling stories, but what I'm saying is, I'm so glad he came to me. I'm so glad I came here. I'm so glad that you're getting better and we'll have years and years to get to know each other. I'm so glad to find out I have a sister. I'm just—"

"Glad?" Ned said with just the right bit of humor that we all started laughing.

I nodded. "Yes."

"That was very Pollyanna-esque," Piper said. And I'd read the books and knew she was talking about *Pollyanna's Glad Game.* "But I understand what you're saying."

"I'm not sure I do," Ned said looking helplessly at the two of them.

"I'm saying thank you, Ned. Thank you for giving me the nudge I needed to be here. Piper will never mention having you in the doghouse again because you saved her life—"

"You saved her life," he interrupted.

"No. I'm here because you came to get me. I'm here because you gave me the kick I needed, like Jaylin did so many years ago. Piper's here because you loved her enough to do what needed to be done. You gave us both a gift, and I think Piper agrees that we'll never be able to repay you for that."

He still looked confused but finally said, "Well, you're welcome, especially since I'm not in the doghouse anymore."

Piper and I both laughed. And finally Ned joined in.

"Your father sent me a picture of you as a toddler in a green bucket and said to ask you to explain."

I could do a better job at this story. "Mom always said I tried to cram as much as possible into every day, which explained, to her way of thinking, why I fell asleep so often in odd places. At the dinner table. In shopping carts. I was pretending the bucket was a pool. When we looked at the photo albums and we'd come to that one, she'd say, *It wasn't much of a pool, but who was I to argue.* I fell asleep, and when she tried to move me to bed, I cried, so she left me there. I took an hour-long nap in that bucket. Well, when she told the story it was an hour. Dad embellishes. These days when he tells it, it was all night."

I continued telling Piper stories for another hour, when she finally dozed off.

Ned and I tiptoed out of the room and I hugged him. "I meant what I said, thank you. You've given me a marvelous gift, the chance to know you all and be a part of this family."

"Thanks for what you said," he countered.

"I think she's going to be all right."

He nodded. "Me, too. I know there are still complications that could arise, and I know that nothing in life's for certain, but I think so. And I know that no matter what happens, having you back in her life matters."

"Dad talked about hearts being elastic. He's right. Mine has stretched and allowed you all in it, and you fit quite nicely. So nicely that I can hardly remember a time you weren't there with the other people I love."

"You say you don't have a way with words but that was almost Pip-esque," he teased.

"And that was a huge compliment." I hugged him. I didn't worry about it being right or loving him too soon. I simply hugged him.

"I'm going to go home, and I'll get Fiona after school," I told him. "Take your time today. I should mention that I have to think about heading home soon. Dad and Margo are packing up the house and need my help and—"

"We're all so grateful you were able to stay this long."

"I'll be back so often you'll be begging for a break."

He shook his head. "Never. You've got a home here."

I stripped off my gown and pulled the charm bracelet out of my pocket. I didn't wear it under the gown because it was cumbersome, and I figured it was probably covered with germs.

"I finished Piper's journal, and that's what you said in your letter." I set the bracelet on the small table and tried the latch.

Ned took it from me and put it on. "I meant it. You will always have a home with us. And I need you to know, it's not just the fact you helped—"

I put my hand on his arm. "I know that."

He nodded. "Even when you're back in Ohio, you'll always have a home with us."

I know I should have said something to that, but I couldn't. I just nodded and walked out of the room.

Piper was getting better. It was time for me to think about heading home.

I spent the afternoon working. I felt guilty that I'd let everything fall to the wayside the last month. Jaylin and I texted back and forth about the project.

Hurricane Fi will be here soon. I'm wrapping up. I'll finish it tonight.

I've got it. And don't apologize.

I laughed because that was what I'd been about to do.

She ended with, *We'll talk tomorrow.*

I sat on the porch, waiting for Fiona. Her red hair made it easy to spot her as she walked down the sidewalk. She waved when she saw me. I waved back. After the crossing guard got her to our side of the street, she sprinted. "Did you see her?" she asked breathlessly.

"I did. And I think she had more color in her cheeks."

"Dad said she's still gets tired easily and still can get sick easy, but she's better. If her numbers keep rising, she can come home soon. She'll need to stick to our house and not go out. And I'll have to still be careful around her 'cause I'm a kid and get germs from school, but she'd be home."

"Speaking of home, I need to head back to mine. Maybe next week. Dad's starting to pack up the house, and I promised to help, and I have to get back to a regular work schedule."

Fiona gave me a look that was so much older than her years. "It's okay, Ban. You'll come back and visit, and when Mom's better, I'm going to come stay with you. Yeah, I know, you're wondering how you got so lucky. I figure we have a lot of sister stuff still to do. And when you're gone, I'll probably text you so much you'll get sick of me."

I laughed. "Never happen."

"Be careful, I might think that's a challenge."

I laughed and I listened to her chatter along happily as she did her homework and I made her dinner. Afterward, I took her to the hospital to see Piper. I didn't gown up this time but waved at Piper through the window.

An hour later, I got a text.

This is the first of a multitude of texts I'll be sending you. Spell-check tried to make multitude multiply the first time 'cause I spelled it wrong. Spell-check is my nemesis.

Mine, too.

Supercalifragilisticexpialidocious. Take that, spell-check.

159

I laughed.

For the next three hours, my phone would beep as Fiona sent other attempts at annoying spell-check.

Finally, right before ten she texted, *Tired of me yet?*

Never, I reassured her.

Indupitably. Spell-check doesn't know how to spell it.

Indubitably, I sent back.

See, sisters are more handy than spell-check. Night.

Night.

It seemed lonely after Fiona's bedtime. I'd miss seeing her every day after I went home. I'd miss Logan, too. And as I had the thought, he walked in the door.

"Hi," I said.

"Hi, yourself," he said. "I checked on Ms. Pip before I came home, and she's still doing great."

"Good," I said.

"Siobhan, why are you looking at me like that?" he asked as he stripped off his scrub shirt.

"Like what?" I asked, wishing he'd strip off more.

"Like that." His eyes narrowed and he nodded, as if that were enough to explain.

I laughed. "I was looking at you like that because I was just thinking about what a good day it was and how happy I was when you walked in. And then I thought how very much I want to take you up to bed."

"I need to shower," he said.

"How about I help you with that?"

We walked up the stairs, and I realized how much I'd miss this when I went home. Not *this. Him.* How much I'd miss Logan.

But I'd let him go because I cared about him.

Caring about someone means putting their needs in front of yours. And he needed to leave.

But he'd be taking a bit of my heart with him when he went.

I knew that because I'd be leaving it here with him when I went home.

Part three: November

Chapter Eleven

Words have power. They can cut, but they can also heal. They can hurt, but they can also uplift.

But maybe even more than words themselves, names have power. If a rock weren't called a rock, would it be as strong? If a cloud weren't a cloud, what would it be? If I weren't my mother's daughter, would I still be me?

—*The Naming of Things*, by Pip

Piper came home from the hospital. Her recovery wasn't over, but she was on the road. All her lab reports were positive. There was no sign of the cancer, and there were signs that her immune system was improving. She had to stay close to home, limit visitors, and take time to recover, but it looked as if she would recover.

I'd finished reading her journal. I'd gone through the trunk. I wore my locket daily and wore the charm bracelet on occasion.

I was wearing it and carrying the journal as I walked through the hole in the fence and let myself in the back door into the kitchen. I no longer knocked. Piper was sitting at the counter. She smiled as I walked in.

"I came to say good-bye. Fiona came over before school, so I already told her." That had been messy. She'd hugged me and

165

cried. I'd promised to come back this month, and she'd asked if she could text me. I'd said anytime. I'd already had three texts. I would not be losing touch with my little sister.

Piper nodded. "She got up early so she could. She's going to miss you. We're all going to miss you." She didn't say the words as a recrimination; she simply said them as a statement of fact.

I knew what she meant. "Me too. I know it's only been a few months, but . . ."

Piper smiled, nodding. "It's the same for me."

"And I'll be back to visit soon," I promised. "Dad and Margo are packing up the house, and I promised to help. Rumor has it I still have some of my childhood toys and stuff in the attic and—"

"You don't have to apologize or make excuses, Siobhan. You're an adult. You have your own life. I'm just so thankful that now I'll get to be a part of it, even in just a little way."

"There's no *little* about it. You are a part of my life. So are Ned and Fiona. You're part of me. I felt guilty at how quickly I loved you and felt a part of you, but as I finished the journal and read Ned's letter talking about why it took him so long to figure out he loved you . . ."

I opened the journal that I'd brought for just this reason.

Why didn't I recognize that last part at first? It seems that I should have known it a lot sooner.

Josiah said it was as obvious to him as the nose on his face.

I've thought a lot about that and realized that I didn't realize it sooner because she was a part of me. Pip was a part of me before I'd even met her. So there was no shock of recognition, no moment when I thought, there she is. I've found her.

166

She'd always been a part of me, and when I finally realized that, I realized what that meant. She never filled a void in my life because she'd always occupied that space. Sort of like a nose.

You have one. You see it every day in the mirror, but you've probably never really stopped and looked and thought, that is my nose. You never ask where you would be without it because it's always been with you, and you know that it always will be with you. You're used to seeing yourself with it. It's simply part of your reflection.

I'm pretty sure that's where the expression originated. And my loving Pip was as obvious as the nose on my face, it was harder to see because it was like a nose.

I closed the journal.

"Ned said it all. You guys are a part of me, like my nose. It didn't take me as long as Ned to figure it out is all," I said with a laugh. "I plan to remind him of that fact often. So I'll come visit, and maybe when you're up to it, you can come to see me. And we'll Skype and text and talk . . ."

I threw my arms around Piper. There was no guilt in loving her. My dad was right. My heart had adapted to its new configuration. There was no guilt. No turmoil. No angst.

There was only love.

Just to be sure Piper understood that, I said, "I love you."

She hugged me back and said, "I love you, too. I have always loved you. You've always been a part of me—"

"Like the nose on your face," I finished, quoting Ned. "He said he wasn't the family writer, but I think he wrote exactly what I needed to hear."

"Better not tell him that. Next thing you know he'll try to help me with my books. He's tried to give me ideas in the past—they weren't good."

I laughed and hugged her again for good measure. She still felt thin, too thin. But I saw beneath her body to the indomitable spirit it held.

Piper said, "I'm thinking about a new story. It's been a year since I've even entertained the idea of a book. I said it was because I was too sick to write, but it was more than that. I didn't want to squander what time I had left on fictional characters. I wanted to concentrate on the real people in my life. Maybe the fact I'm thinking about a new book means I'm feeling well enough to believe I've got enough time for fictional characters *and* the real people in my life. Soon I'll be going back to Amanda's Pantry. I feel like I have a future."

She hesitated. "When you came back, you brought back a piece of my heart that's been missing all these years. You and your father have given me the gift of stories from your childhood. And now, you've given me more time with the people I love, and you've given me back my writing. Thank you."

I felt as if I was going to cry and didn't want to leave Piper with tears, so I said, "I better go. Logan'll be home soon, and I can tell him good-bye as well."

"Will you text me when you get home so I don't worry?"

I might have laughed, but I knew Piper had spent a lifetime worrying about me. Giving that up might be hard. "Definitely. And I'll be back soon."

She nodded.

I walked back through the now autumn-brittle garden. I swear that it smelled like snow. We'd had some frosts but not snow yet, though I knew it was coming. November hit the lakeshore suddenly and frequently with a vengeance.

I walked to the bench at the back of the garden. It was Piper's favorite thinking spot, and over the last few months it had become mine as well.

The milkweed was now nothing more than wooden stalks. They rustled in the breeze, a lighter sound than the branches. I closed my eyes and simply listened. Fiona's birds were at the feeder. I could hear them chirping back and forth.

I wondered how many would winter here and how many, like me, were moving on.

I opened my eyes and saw two blue jays were at the feeder. A group of jays is called a band. I wasn't sure if I'd ever told Fiona that one.

I pulled out my phone and texted her. *A group of blue jays is called a band. Just thought of it, which made me think of you.*

She didn't answer, which was good, since she should be in class about now and shouldn't have her phone on. The text would be waiting for her.

I looked toward the house.

When I'd arrived, I hadn't been able to see it from here, but now that all the plants had died off and the trees had lost all their leaves, it was visible.

Piper was sitting in the kitchen. Later, she'd probably move to the chair near the front window. She wasn't feeling well enough to write yet, but she was thinking about it.

I'd read all her books now. All the stories I'd missed. I was anxious to add to my collection.

I got up and headed back to the house. I'd packed my bags. I'd washed the sheets and remade the bed. There was nothing left to do but say good-bye to Logan.

I heard the front door open as I came in the back. I went out to the front. He was looking at my suitcases as he stood there in his stained scrubs. I didn't ask with what. I didn't want to know.

"I was in the ER last night," he said, by way of explanation. "It was a rough shift."

I nodded. "I'm sorry."

"You're leaving then?" he asked.

I nodded. "Yes. I just waited to say good-bye and to thank you for letting me stay here."

"It's Ned's house," he said, trying to deflect my gratitude.

But we both knew that I wasn't simply thanking him for sharing the roof over our heads but for so much more. "Thank you for being my . . ."

I didn't know what to call our relationship, so I said, "Thanks for being here for me. I'm not sure how I'd have gotten through it without you."

I thought about all the mornings I'd woken up in his arms. The way he'd nursed me after the surgery.

His smiley face underwear.

He smiled. "Anytime."

"So, I'll see you when I visit, I'm sure."

"You're always welcome to stay here," he said. "Well, as long as I'm here."

"Thanks." I looked at his stained scrubs and added, "I'd hug you but . . ."

The stains were a good excuse not to hug him. On the heels of that thought I asked myself, why was I hesitant to hug him? We'd become friends and lovers. That's what I was to him, but he was more than that to me. That's why I didn't hug him.

"Yeah, I wouldn't hug me, either," he said with a happy smile, though beneath the expression I thought I saw something else. Something that didn't look happy at all. "It was a messy night at work."

I thought leaving Piper would be hard, but I felt as if we'd said everything we needed to say. And I knew she'd always be a part of my life. Logan wouldn't be. Oh, I'd see him when I visited, until he finished school next spring and left. Then who knew if our paths would ever cross again.

I drank in one last sight of him, and then I picked up my bag. "Well, good-bye."

"Drive safe," he said.

I nodded and walked out the door, trying to ignore the thought that our good-bye was wrong. I should have done something else, but I wasn't sure what.

The drive back to Ohio was uneventful. The skiy looked ominous, but all the weatherman's dire threats of snow didn't come to anything.

I pulled into my driveway and waited for that feeling of coming home. But it never came.

I pulled my bigger suitcase with me up onto the porch and let myself into the house. No dog came running to greet me. No nine-year-old redhead screamed my name. No Piper. No Ned.

No Logan.

As if she knew I was thinking about her, Fiona texted. *Cool. A group of finches is a charm.*

A second later another text beeped.

I miss you.

I miss you, too, I texted back.

I stuffed the phone in my back pocket and simply stood in the foyer for a moment. My house felt very big and lonely.

Then I heard a noise.

"Who's there?" I called and almost immediately wished I hadn't. It was dumb to announce your presence to robbers. I started to open the front door so I could step out and call the cops, when Carey called out, "Ban, is that you?"

He stepped out of my living room.

171

"Carey? What are you doing here?"

"I . . ."

And then I knew. "You've been staying here?"

"I stayed with my parents but then moved in with Mark for a couple of weeks, but then he said I needed to get out and I had nowhere to go. Mom and Dad told me I couldn't move back in unless I got a job. I told them I was trying. Dad said there was a job in the shop, but I am not starting at the bottom. I have a college degree. So they said no. What was I supposed to do?"

"Here's the thing, I don't care. My suggestion would be pack your stuff and tell your dad *yes, please*, but that's up to you. You have exactly ten minutes to get your stuff and get out. Ten minutes or I'm calling the cops."

"Ban, I—"

I pulled out my cell phone, opened the timer app, and set it for ten minutes. Then I turned it so Carey could see.

"I'm not kidding."

He didn't whine. He looked at me and obviously finally saw what I was saying.

He was wheeling his suitcase down the stairs when the timer rang.

"Give me the key, and if you have any other spares, I want them, too."

"I don't." He dug in his pocket and handed me a key.

"Good-bye, Carey."

He didn't say anything as he wheeled his suitcase to the sidewalk. He sat on it and got out a phone.

I'll confess, I stood at the window and watched. Fifteen minutes later, his father came and got him.

I turned from the window and looked back at the house.

It felt . . . different.

I decided that finding Carey here had somehow tainted it. Rather than stick around and wait for the house to settle back into itself, I left my suitcase where it stood, threw the deadbolt in place, got back in the car, and headed for Dad and Margo's.

I drove past my old neighborhood on the way and parked for a moment in front of the house I grew up in. There was no front porch, but I knew that around back there was a big deck.

Every year Mom and Dad threw an end-of-the-school-year barbecue. The yard was big for a Port Clinton yard, but when I remembered the teachers and their families in it, it was full. Mom was always smiling as she talked to her friends, all of them sharing stories of the school year like old combat buddies sharing war stories.

I loved those parties because I knew that the next day our summer adventures would begin. Having parents who were teachers gave me a unique summer experience.

It wasn't simply vacations, though those were sweet. It was lazy days, when the three of us sat quietly reading books. It was trips for ice cream. It was laughter and trips to the lake.

The small Cape Cod house with the bright blue shutters that used to be gray had been my home for eighteen years. But even as the old memories came back, I realized that it wasn't home any more. Not without Mom and Dad there.

I started my car and didn't look back at it as I drove to Dad's new house.

I studied Dad and Margo's condo a minute before I got out. It was a contemporary-looking condo with its dark wood siding and floor-to-ceiling windows. As I walked to the door, I realized that though I'd never lived in it, this was home. This was the feeling I'd been waiting for.

"You're back," Dad said as he opened the door and hugged me.

"I am." I was surprised to see boxes piled up in the hall.

He saw me look at them and smiled. "We put the condo on the market, and it sold the next day. So we're packing up everything and putting it in storage until the end of the term, when we move."

"Wow. That was fast."

He nodded. "Margo said it's like pulling a bandage . . . it's easier if you do it all at once. I was just going to pack your stuff with ours, but since you're here, maybe you want to look at what you have, and see if you want any of it."

I nodded. "I should have taken it when you and Margo moved to the condo."

"There wasn't that much," he said. "And we have a huge attic here."

I hugged him, just because I could. "Love you," I said.

He smiled. "I know, honey. I love you, too. How was Piper?"

"Better," I said. "I think being home has made a huge difference. She's thinking about writing again."

"That's good."

"It is. Logan told me that he remembers her sitting on her porch in the nice weather, or in the window when it was cold, with her laptop on her lap. He said all the kids loved seeing her work. I realized that I'd like to see that."

"It might take time, but I've read her books. She won't stop."

"She said she'd put it aside when she got sick again because she wanted to concentrate on real people, not on fictional ones. The fact that she's thinking about writing means she trusts she'd have enough time for both." I blinked back tears as I said the words.

Dad didn't say anything, he just nodded that he understood. We stopped in the upstairs hall, where there was a pile of five boxes.

I opened the first one. Barbies, one of whom was ever so bald. "Do you remember when I wanted to be a beautician? I thought I'd cut Barbie's hair."

Dad laughed. "Afterward, we encouraged you to find some other career."

I laughed as I dug around in the box. "My Noah's ark. I had more fun with this set, though I always—"

"Hated that the animals were not proportional to one another," Dad finished.

"Seriously, the rabbit's almost as big as the tiger. I want to know what zoo the designer went to for his inspiration."

There was nothing of earth-shattering importance, but I knew I'd be taking all the boxes home with me.

I was digging through the second one when I asked Dad, "Won't you miss home?"

"I'll be honest, home is wherever Margo is. I know it sounds like something on a greeting card, but there it is. Home, at least for me, is where the heart is. She's my home. And so are you. Wherever you live will be my home, too."

I pulled out an ugly plastic troll. He'd been a multipurpose troll. Sometimes he went on the ark and played Japheth, one of Noah's sons, and sometimes he dated Barbie. I mean, she had such a bad hairdo, she hadn't minded his trollish spikes.

"You can only have one home," I said without looking up.

Dad's laughter made me drop my troll and look at him as he said, "Honey, that's like saying you can only love one person. You can have many homes. Wherever someone you love is, that's home."

As he said the words, an image of Logan flashed through my mind.

I picked up my Dorothy doll in her ruby-red slippers. It struck me as rather apropos. I felt like I'd tapped my heels together and finally realized what I'd known all along. I'd worried that I'd fallen in love with Piper, Ned, and Fiona too fast. But Ned was right, they were like the nose on my face. I'd admitted that Logan was in my elastic heart with everyone else, but I'd never said the words.

I loved him.

Piper said love happens in its own way, in its own time. Ned said that it took him a long time to realize Piper was a part of him. He realized there was no sudden moment of realization because he'd always loved her. Even my dad had said something like that. Love just is. Home isn't a place; it's people.

My phone dinged and I opened a text from Fiona.

A group of starlings is a murmuration.

I started to laugh and held up the phone so dad could read it. He smiled. "You've infected your sister with your odd affinity for weird names."

Suddenly, it was as clear as the nose on my face what I had to do next.

I got the name of Dad's moving company and real estate agent and packed up my house over the next few days.

As I pulled out of the driveway a week later, the agent was pounding a For Sale sign into the front lawn.

I didn't feel any twinges of regret at leaving this home. Instead, I felt excited and ready to get back home. I knew that leaving home to go home might not make sense to someone else, but it made every bit of sense to me.

I was going home.

Less than three hours later, I pulled up in front of the houses across from the school in Erie, Pennsylvania. A few snowflakes landed on my windshield. I'd made it home before the snow. That was good.

I felt myself tear up when I saw that Piper and Ned were sitting on the porch. She not only had a winter coat and hat on, but she was bundled up and wrapped in a blanket as well. I was sure that the blanket was Ned's doing. She'd probably wanted to see the first snow, and Ned couldn't say no. But he could make sure she was bundled up.

Seeing them on the front porch was very much a sign.

"Siobhan," Piper said. She started to get up, but I waved her back to her seat. "What are you doing here?"

"I'm home." I smiled as I said the words. "You said you'd always dreamed that when I came home, you'd be on the front porch waiting for me. I'm so glad you're here now."

"I don't understand," she said.

Ned didn't say anything, but I saw that he did understand, and he reached out and took my hand.

"I'm hoping that you'll let me crash next door again for a bit. My house in Port Clinton's officially on the market. I'll find a real estate agent here in town and start looking for a house as soon as it sells. But I was hoping I could stay next door while I wait. All my things are in storage. I know it was a bit cheeky to assume—"

"Wait," Piper said. "You're moving to Erie?"

"Yes. Dad and Margo are leaving for Atlanta over the Christmas break, and without them there, Port Clinton's not my home anymore. Home's not a place; it's the people that you love. I'll always have a home with them, but I have one here, too. And I think I need to be here for now. I want to spend time with you and Fiona and—"

Piper didn't let me get any further. She got out of her chair and wrapped me in her arms. "Welcome home, Siobhan."

"I love you," I said.

Ned got up as well and hugged us both. Suddenly, Fiona was on the porch. She threw down her school bag and joined the group hug. "Why are we hugging and crying?" she asked.

"Siobhan's moving home," Ned said.

"For good?" she asked me.

"For now," I said. Because if I had my way, there was a chance that Erie wasn't the only home I was going to make.

Piper seemed to sense what I was thinking. She sat back down and said, "He's working until eleven."

"I guess he's in for a surprise when he gets home tonight."

"Hey, Ban, did you know that a group of turtledoves is known as a pitying?" Fiona asked.

We all laughed.

I was home.

I borrowed Piper's idea and was wrapped in a quilt at just after eleven, waiting for Logan.

The little bit of snow earlier hadn't stuck around, but there were thick clouds overhead, obliterating any hope of seeing the moon or the stars. The atmosphere felt charged with anticipation. I wasn't sure if it was the weather gearing up for more snow or me gearing up for Logan getting home.

There were a few lights on in the school. Probably the cleaning crew.

It was quiet out. The birds had long since tucked themselves away for the night. The lights were off next door as well.

I'd stayed for dinner. Fiona kept us all in stitches as she recited different bird group names. As I was leaving, I asked her if she'd memorized a list. She'd told me that every time she missed me, she looked up another group. Then very seriously she said, "I missed you a lot."

I'd missed her, too.

It felt right being here. I needed to find a house and get settled and get back to work. Jaylin had gone above and beyond picking up the slack for me. I was working every day again, but I owed her a hundred percent, and I wasn't sure I'd even reached eighty.

My phone binged.

A kettle of raptors, Fiona said.

Go to sleep.

Night.

A car pulled in the drive. Even with just the streetlight for illumination, I hungrily drank in the sight of him. He smiled when he saw me and hurried onto the porch. "I thought you were going home."

I stood up and tucked my phone in my back pocket, leaving both my hands free as I hugged him. I pulled back and looked at him. "Have I ever mentioned I have a very poor sense of direction?"

He looked confused but happy to see me. "No, you never mentioned it."

I nodded and tried to keep a serious expression. "I do. You see, for a while I thought home was west of here, in Port Clinton. Then I thought it was east of Port Clinton in Erie. I was a bit turned around, you see. But I always get to the right destination, even if it takes me a while." But not as long as it had taken Ned, I reminded myself.

Logan looked confused. "What do you mean?"

"Home isn't a place. It's people. And I've learned a very important lesson. It's possible to have more than one home. I have one with Dad and Margo. And I have a home with Piper, Ned, and Fiona. And I think there's a chance I have a home with you."

He shook his head. "I don't have a home. I travel the world. I'm already signed up to go away next summer," he said. I wasn't sure if he was reminding me or reminding himself.

"You're not listening to what I'm saying—home isn't a place; it's people. Dad and Margo are my people. Piper, Ned, and Fiona are my people. Jaylin is my people. And you, Logan—you are my people. Even if you don't think I'm your people, you're mine. You are home. We've only known each other for a few months, I get that. Frankly, the fact I've known you for such a short time scared me. But I've learned a lot in the last few months. I've learned enough that my heart recognizes home when it sees it. When I look at you, I'm home."

"But I travel the world . . ."

"And I have a very portable job. As long as we can find me an Internet connection, I'm good."

"But—"

I cut him off. I realized that just because I'd figured things out for me that didn't mean he had. "Listen, if this is too fast or too much, I get that. If you're not inclined, I can accept that, too. But, Logan, don't use your job as an excuse—just tell me thanks but no thanks. Let's face it; there are sick and needy people everywhere. I think Piper proves that."

"So what you're saying is . . . ," he prompted.

I'd hoped he'd give me some clue about what he felt, but even without it, I said, "I love you, you dolt."

"I love you, too." He paused a moment and said, "Welcome home."

He didn't say a word but took my hand in his and led me upstairs. When we got upstairs, he finally saw what I'd been wearing.

"Smiley face pajama pants?"

"I bought underwear as well, but I wasn't about to sit outside in those."

He laughed and pulled me into his arms.

I was home.

Epilogue

Your heart has infinite room. You never run out of room to love one more person. They'll simply move in one day and make themselves at home . . . sometimes without you even noticing.
—*The Naming of Things*, by Pip

"It's good to be home," I said.

Logan smiled at me. "I never leave home anymore."

I must have looked at him blankly because he laughed and said, "Home is where the heart is and all that. A wise woman told me as much."

I laughed. That seemed to be the theme of our lives together. Love and laughter.

We drove down Peach Street, as we had so many times. We'd just left Dad and Margo's. They'd moved into a condo in Atlanta, and while I knew I'd always have a home with them, Erie had become my home as well. More specifically, the small house I shared with Logan just east of State Street. It was within walking distance of Piper and Ned's.

But today, instead of driving to our house, Logan drove to Piper's. It looked the same as ever, though this year the garden seemed to have crept even farther into Ned's backyard. Piper and Ned had lent his house out to the Beaumont family, a single mom with three kids. We'd met them before this trip with First Aid.

181

We pulled up in front of the house, and there was Piper in her chair. She had on holey jeans, her legs propped up on a stool, her laptop balanced on top of them. The purple flower teacup was on the stand next to her. She smiled and waved as Fi came bolting out of the house and ran past her mom—our mom—to the car. "Where is she?" she demanded.

"Logan, do you get the feeling that we've lost some ground in Fi's esteem? I mean, no, hey-Logan, or hi-sis. Just *where is she?*"

Fiona laughed. "Yeah, I still love you both, but I've had you guys like forever. I want to get my hands on Talia Rose before Mom—"

"I can hear you Fi Marie," Piper called. She was tapping keys on her laptop. I assumed she was closing down her work.

"You were meant to, 'cause once you get her, I don't stand a chance."

I opened the back door of the car and started to unbuckle Talia from her car seat. She woke up and blinked a few times and then smiled. Smiling was Talia's default expression.

She was eleven months old now and was walking—well, more like running—everywhere.

"What happened to her eye?" Fi asked as I handed Talia to her aunt.

"She got into a wrestling match with the coffee table, and the coffee table won." My daughter had an indomitable spirit. She had Logan's eyes—a bluish gray that would always remind me of Lake Erie. But she had my hair. I took solace in the fact my hair was also Piper and Fiona's hair.

It was a much more tangible connection than mitochondrial DNA.

"Hey, T. R.," Fi said. "Come back into the garden. Papa made you a playhouse. It's got . . ." Fi's voice got lower as they disappeared along the side of the house and through the gate.

"We won't see her again," Logan said.

"At least not until she needs a diaper change. Fiona still proclaims quite loudly that aunts don't change diapers. Last I heard, Piper was working on a book called *Ants Don't Change Pants*."

"I am," Piper said. "I think it's going to be the first of a new series. I've got a little rhyme in it."

Talia Rose,
where do you suppose
the sun goes to at night?

It goes to sleep
in the boughs of the trees,
when I go to bed at night.

Talia Rose,
where do you suppose
the flowers go in the snow?

To sleep in the dirt,
where the cold won't hurt,
that's where they go when it snows.

Talia Rose,
where do you suppose
my love goes every day?

It's in my heart
when we're apart . . .
It's in my hair,
in the rocks and the air.
It's in the sky
and the clouds and your eyes . . .

Piper shrugged. "It's a work in progress."

"It's beautiful."

"So's our T. R. Do you suppose I have a chance at getting a few hugs in?"

"You're going to have to fight Fi for a turn," I warned.

"Then why don't we go back into the garden? I feel up to that wrestling match." She raked a finger through her short, thick hair. It had grown in with two very prominent streaks of gray, but they made her look distinguished.

As we walked, she took my hand. Logan opened the garden gate, and we stepped into the garden.

I saw Ned tossing Talia up into the air. Both the baby and Fiona laughed as I stood between my husband and my Piper.

I worried for a long time about what to call her. I didn't worry any more. I realize that the naming of things mattered, and I had accepted that I had many names for Piper. Birth mother, friend, family. Now she was grandmother to my daughter.

But what mattered most was that Piper was *home*.

I took Logan's hand in mine.

"Welcome home, Talia Rose," Fiona cried.

"Welcome home," I whispered.

Note from the Author

January 2016

Dear Reader,

I love exploring the question of what makes a family. There is a never-ending supply of answers. Sometimes a family is made through genetics, but so often families are born through other paths. Adoption, marriage, friendship . . .

I think that the core answer to that question is that a family is always made through love. That's one of the truths that Siobhan has to discover. The other truth is there is no such thing as a heart that's filled to capacity. There's always room for one more. And finally, she realizes that home isn't a physical place . . . home is wherever there are people you love.

My kids are getting older and making their own homes. But as they've left to start their own lives, I've never felt sad because I know that wherever I am, they will always still have a home with me, too.

I hope readers who met Piper and Ned in *Carry Her Heart* enjoyed revisiting them ten years down the line. When I closed *Carry Her Heart*, they were beginning their own happily ever after. And maybe seeing them both suffering through Pip's illness doesn't seem like I delivered on that promise. But I think I did. Because though Pip's sick, we see that their relationship is still strong. If anything, it's become stronger because of her illness. They have Fiona, along with their friends and family. And after ten years of waiting, they have Siobhan.

Maybe that's one of the points of the story. Life comes with hurdles. Sometimes just little bumps in the roads; sometimes tsunamis. But if we have people we love surrounding us and supporting us, there can be happiness even in the midst of pain. That's what Piper and Ned have found. And that's what Siobhan and Logan have found as well. Having someone who loves you completely, well that is a gift that can see you through the good times and the bad.

I do want to acknowledge that I talked with medical consultants about Pip's illness, and I know I might have fudged the timeline on her transplant and homecoming, but I didn't fudge anything when I talked about how many people are waiting for a gift of life like Siobhan was able to give Piper. And my hat's off to everyone who's been tested and has added their name to the registry. That kind of generosity of spirit is amazing.

I hope you enjoyed *Hold Her Heart*! Some of you might have spotted a cameo from a character in *These Three Words*. If so, keep an eye out, Alice, the nurse in that story, has her own book coming out soon.

If you're a new reader, thank you so much for giving one of my stories a try. As always, I want to thank all of you so much for your continued support!

Holly

www.HollyJacobs.com

About the Author

Award-winning author Holly Jacobs has sold almost three million books worldwide. The first novel in her Everything But . . . series, *Everything But a Groom*, was named one of 2008's Best Romances by *Booklist*, and her books have been honored with countless other accolades.

Holly has a wide range of interests, from her love for writing to gardening and even basket weaving. She has delivered more than sixty author workshops and keynote speeches across the country. She lives in Erie, Pennsylvania, with her family and her dogs. She frequently sets stories in and around her hometown.